FIRE . . .

Flames licked up, red-tipped, yellow and gold, they rose beneath me. Twin agonies: fire and fear of fire. I was going to burn. I was going to burn alive.

Flames raced up the tree's trunk, unnatural fire, too fast, too fast, too swiftly advancing. Up the trunk to stop just below David. Along the branches, as though someone had splashed the branches with gasoline.

I hear screams, inhuman and human. The demons danced in the flames, happy in their element. They filled their hands with fire and washed their faces with it and laughed at us screaming and crying and begging.

David's voice was a harsh bellow. Again and again. Or was that me? Some awful sound was coming from me, some sound I could never have willed, some sound that was squeezed from the darkest corners of my mind.

I choked on the smoke, on the demon's filth, on my own terror. *Let the smoke take me,* I begged, *let the smoke take me now, don't let me burn alive. . . .*

D0197623

Look for other EVERWORLD titles

by K.A. Applegate:

EVER WORLD

BRAVE THE BETRAYAL

K. A. APPLEGATE

SCHOLASTIC INC.
New York Toronto London Auckland Sydney
Mexico City New Delhi Hong Kong

ISBN 0-590-87854-9

12 11 10 9 8 7 6 5 4 3 2 1   0 1 2 3 4 5/0

Printed in the U.S.A.

First Scholastic printing, July 2000

For Michael and Jake

BRAVE THE BETRAYAL

CHAPTER I

"Miyuki. Her name is Miyuki."

"Me-you-key?" Christopher sounded it out.

"Yeah. That's right."

"You going to be able to say that in a moment of passion? Oh, oh, baby, oh, Miyuki?"

I said, "It means 'deep snow.' In Japanese." I knew it was a bad idea to tell Christopher that, but I went right ahead and did it anyway.

"Deep snow." He nodded. "That, my friend, is the girl for you: deep yet cold."

"I don't think you should read too much into a name. Your name means 'person with Christ in his heart.' My name means 'Godlike.'"

"Hmm. You make a good point there, Jalil. And she is a babe. At least her face. I can't see the rest of her. She has a body, right? I mean, over there under the table? Paint me the picture."

"No. I am not going to paint you a picture."

"Then you leave me no choice but to leer at your One True Love when she gets up to leave."

"You would do that anyway."

Christopher grinned, revealing a piece of lettuce that I really didn't need to see. "I can't deny that. I assume if you're interested in her she must be some kind of genius."

"Look how she eats. These neat, tiny bites. She can eat a taco and still not make a mess."

Christopher gave me a look, like he wasn't sure what I thought I was talking about. "Well, she has a small mouth."

The two of us were at the Taco Bell near campus. Lunch. The place was jammed with kids from school, plus a few workmen from the crew that was repaving the road and tying up traffic.

It was loud in Taco Bell. People ordering and people taking orders, paper crumpling, ice sloshing, plastic trays clattering, laughter, groans, yells, shouts.

And it was hot. It's a fact of life that the colder it gets outside the hotter it gets inside. People feel the need to crank the thermostat despite the fact that when it's cold outside people are going to be wearing coats, so the last thing they need is for it to be ninety degrees inside.

Today the windows with their painted-on announcements of ninety-nine-cent burritos were dripping condensation. People sloughed off their puffy jackets and tried to hang them on the backs of their seats. It all made the place even more crowded.

Miyuki was not sweating. Deep snow. In fact she was smiling at one of the other girls at her table. Nice smile. Sweet, that was the word for it. Christopher was right, she did have a small mouth.

If I was any kind of a man I'd just do it and get it over with, I told myself. She knew who I was. We were the only two nonseniors taking advanced calculus. So it's not like she didn't know who I was. It's not like I would be some complete stranger asking her out.

"Go ahead," Christopher said, as though he'd just read my thoughts. "You're in the Geekhood together. Just flash her your secret geek hand gesture and use the word 'inchoate' in a sentence. She'll leap into your arms and start conjugating Latin verbs."

I took a bite of burrito. At that very moment Miyuki looked over at me and smiled. Or maybe she was looking at someone behind me.

I couldn't smile back. I had a mouthful of beans and hamburger. I probably wouldn't have smiled anyway. I have a smile, I'm capable of it — it's just not the first thing I think of. I'm not an automatic smiler. My default face involves frowning and looking a little bothered.

"She wants you," Christopher said, drumming his fingers in a way that made his boredom clear. "You could cut the sexual tension in here with a knife. One of those limp little plastic knives."

"You know, you'd think with all we're dealing with over there, I'd be braver about little stuff," I said. "I mean, it's easy, right? 'Hi, Miyuki, I was wondering whether you'd like to go out sometime.' That's not the hardest thing in the world. Is it?"

"Yeah, well, you need to work on your opening line." He thought for a moment, then snapped his fingers. "Lovely Miyuki, your name means 'deep snow,' my name means 'Godlike.' My Godlike powers can melt your snow, baby, no matter how deep, if you know what I mean."

"Yeah, that would be better," I said. "She'd be sure to go for that."

Christopher laughed. Then, in midlaugh, he got a distant, far-off look. I knew the look. He was feeling a vague, undefined sense of loss. Absence. Absence of himself.

I checked my own state of mind. No, I was still

here. Maybe. I couldn't really tell. Not for sure. Sometimes I was right, other times I was wrong.

"You gone?" I asked Christopher.

He shrugged. "I don't know, man. This is messed up. What does it matter? I'm still here even if he's awake."

I took another bite. I stole a covert glance at Miyuki. She had very delicate hands. She seemed very clean.

"What do you think the Egyptian gods will be like?"

"Hard to say," I said. "I read a little about it. They're very confusing. They keep changing identities, kind of melding into one another. Changing attributes. Isis is one of your better-sounding gods, though. Fertility, motherhood, magic. So maybe it won't end up with us screaming."

Christopher nodded glumly. "I'll miss old Dionysus when we go. I wonder if the Egyptians have a party god?"

"Hey, Christopher!" It was some kid I'd never seen before. Maybe he was from our school, but I had a feeling he wasn't. He was a small, hard-looking kid. My first instinct was to think *redneck*.

Christopher was not glad to see him. "What do you want, Keith?"

Keith grinned at me. "Just thought maybe you'd introduce me to your friend here."

He stuck out his hand, let it hover there in the air in front of my face, waiting for me to shake it. I started to reach but saw Christopher give a quick, negative jerk of his head.

"Guess I was right about you, huh, Christopher?" Keith said, withdrawing the hand slowly.

"Yeah," Christopher said evenly. "I guess you were."

Keith seemed a bit confused by that answer, like it wasn't what he'd expected. I could see his mind working, looking for a comeback. But all he managed was, "Just remember to keep your mouth shut."

Then I was awake in my bed, the bed I'd come to think of as mine, anyway. A servant was moving around the room. He opened curtains. Brilliant morning light. Blue sky. There was no glass in the window. We were a couple millennia away from glass windows.

"What's up?" I asked the servant.

He gave me a carefully calibrated bow, a sort of absolute minimum bow, and said, "Wise Athena has requested your presence."

"Oh. Okay." A second servant came in carrying enough food to end a famine. My first thought was that I was full. I'd just eaten a burrito.

But of course that Jalil, and that stomach, and that burrito in that stomach, were a universe away. And here, this Jalil, with this stomach, was hungry.

Christopher filled the doorway. "Guess I was right, huh? I was gone."

II

A visit with Athena was not the worst fate in Everworld.

Athena was the smartest of the gods we'd met. The most stable. But that's only relative to other gods. As a rule, gods are not very bright and have the temperament of any petty dictator. Don't think "gentle Jesus, meek and mild," think Saddam Hussein or Slobodan Milosovic.

Almost all of the gods we'd met personally, or that I'd read about, were casual killers, often serial rapists as well. Their myths — Greek, Roman, Irish, Aztec, Inca, Egyptian, it didn't matter — their stories were loaded up with tales of rape and murder. Murder of men and women and children, rivals, people who had committed minor offenses, people whose looks they didn't like, people who just happened to be standing in the wrong place when the god got grouchy or horny.

Athena, the Greek goddess of wisdom and war, was different. They say she invented the olive tree, the chariot, the potter's wheel. She defended the great heroes: Odysseus, Perseus, Bellerephon.

It's hard to say that we liked her. She was, after all, seven feet tall even when she was at her smallest. She walked around with a spear and a shield, and the decorative motif on her aegis was the decapitated head of a woman with snakes for hair. She could, at a whim, decide to shish-kebab the five of us on her spear. Hard to like anyone who has so much more power than you do.

But. She had saved April's life. And she had backed us in arguments with Zeus and Ares, both genuine head cases. And she tried. She tried, and at times it was almost sad, and it made her sad, I know. Thing was that she alone, of the gods we'd met, knew enough to know her own limitations. She knew she was a prisoner of her own myth.

The five of us — David, Christopher, April, Senna, and I — all ate our fabulous, extravagant breakfasts and put on clean clothes — they'd been washed for us during the night — and were driven in a sedate wagon to Athena's Parthenon, right on Olympus's marble-paved main drag.

There was no mystery about the purpose of the meeting. We had to figure out how to undo our own careless mistake. We weren't exactly the serpents in the Garden of Eden, but we had managed to take a bad situation and make it worse.

We had introduced gunpowder.

Everworld is a universe created separate and apart from our own, by the gods of myth. I guess they felt things were going badly in what they call the old world and we call the real world. So they invented their own little universe. They hauled a bunch of people along with them: the necessary toadies and victims without whom no god ever feels complete. Odin, Zeus, Jupiter, the Daghdha, Quetzalcoatl, and who knows who else all made peace for as long as it took to unite their powers and invent this place.

Everworld operated by their laws. They wrote the software. Call it Windows B.C. Or Windows 999 A.D. I don't know when they did it; I don't even know whether the notion of "when" has any relevance. They did it. That's the fact. They inflated this bubble and let it float free of our old universe with all its stodgy rules about cause and effect, about time only moving in one direction, about equal and opposite reactions.

A lot of the old rules still pertain. But instead of being hard and fast laws, they're like the laws in old-time Chicago: The powerful can disregard them.

I won't try to disguise the fact that this bothers me. I don't like the idea of Everworld. It seems like the gods cheated humanity somehow.

Humans evolved from prehuman primates, formed into small bands and later into villages and later still into cities and nations. And as they gained greater and greater control over their environment, learned to make tools and control fire, and eventually to read and write, they moved into a world where reason played a larger role and superstition a smaller one.

I think that's why Everworld was made. I think the gods saw that the good old Homo sapiens was outgrowing them.

Me, I'm a child of the last gasp of the twentieth and the earliest dawn of the twenty-first century. I like the twenty-first century. I like the light of reason. I don't like being forced back into the darkness.

But the self-labeled gods — whatever they may be in reality — saw their handiwork and decided it was good. Until some immortals from a different neighborhood started crashing the party. Aliens.

To be specific, the gods of different alien species became aware of Everworld and invaded it. An alien invasion that didn't require faster-than-light travel. All they had to do was figure out how to pierce the bubble. The two universes aren't far apart like a pair of galaxies. Distance is irrelevant. Everworld and the real world aren't in space.

The alien gods and their own followers started crowding into Everworld. I don't know how many different species. And they may still be coming. I don't think anyone knows. We've heard a number of them mentioned, but we've only run into two: the Coo-Hatch and the Hetwan.

The Hetwan were the serious problem. Their god, Ka Anor, had what to the local gods seemed a very unpleasant attribute: He ate other gods. The Daghdha, father god of the Celts, was eaten. At least that's what a dragon told us. Other gods as well, though I doubt anyone knows how many. They don't exactly keep careful records in Everworld.

Ganymede was eaten. We saw that, and it was a shame. Ganymede had started life as a mortal, so he had some redeeming characteristics.

It was a terrible thing to see. Terrible to recall. But then that was true of so much in Everworld. There are parts of our time here that I would burn out of my memory if I could. And I don't say that lightly, because I believe in truth, all truth, even the truth that bothers you. But things have happened in Everworld . . . things I don't ever want creeping into my nightmares.

The Coo-Hatch seemed more benign than the Hetwan. They're an odd, melancholy kind of race. They seem to wander, rootless, in little bands of a few dozen members. Their great talent is in the working of metals. They made a kind of steel that was so hard, so incorruptible, so sharp that a man with a Coo-Hatch blade could cut his way through a castle wall.

It was in our first encounter with the Coo-Hatch that we made what now seemed like a fatal error. We traded them one of our few possessions: a chemistry book. In exchange they didn't kill us — we had thought they might. And they replaced the blade of my Swiss Army knife with Coo-Hatch steel.

It is a sweet knife. We call it Excalibur. But the Coo-Hatch got the better of that deal, because within the pages of our chem book they found the basis for making gunpowder.

Combine gunpowder with the greatest metallurgists ever, and you have guns and cannon before you can blink. The Coo-Hatch brought primitive guns to help the Hetwan against Olympus. It was more a warning than a serious attempt to help Ka Anor's buggy boys to take Olympus. The Coo-

Hatch were sending a message. That was our guess, anyway, and we got it.

The Coo-Hatch wanted something, and they wanted it badly, and if they didn't get it the Greek warriors in their leather and pot-metal armor were going to be waving swords at cannonballs. Only one way that kind of thing comes out.

A single captured Coo-Hatch presented their terms: They wanted out of Everworld. I guess the Coo-Hatch were not of the follow-your-gods-no-matter-what type of religion. I liked that about them. They figured their gods had screwed them and after a century trapped in Everworld they wanted to go back home. They wanted Zeus to get them there.

Zeus couldn't. Senna maybe could.

Senna was a real-worlder, like us. Only not like us. She was not just another kid from school.

It pains me to admit this but Senna has powers that should not exist in the real world. Somehow she embodies a crossover between universes. She is stronger in Everworld than in the real world, but even in the real world she seems able to violate the laws of our universe in small ways.

She can change shape and appearance. She can compel desire. She can heal the sick. I know. She healed me, at least for a few moments.

She's a gateway. Some kind of cross-universe

anomaly. That's why Loki kidnapped her — and us along with her. Loki and some other gods are scared to death of Ka Anor and want to escape back to the real world. They want to use Senna to do that. Senna won't play. Not out of any sense of morality — she simply wants to be powerful in her own right.

But Senna claims she doesn't have the power to liberate the Coo-Hatch. She can cross between our universe and Everworld, but not between Everworld and the Coo-Hatch universe.

So she says. But, says Senna, there is someone who can accomplish that feat: her own mother.

And that's why we were meeting with Athena. Because we were supposed to find Senna's mother and convince her to help the Coo-Hatch, which would take the Coo-Hatch out of the Hetwan equation and slow the Hetwan down.

And as confusing as all that is, it barely scratches the surface. We had Loki on our tails looking to snag Senna and murder the rest of us. And we had Merlin chasing us, looking to snag Senna but not murder the rest of us. And while we were at it, we'd managed to make permanent enemies of Huitzilopoctli and Hel, a pair of gods who, respectively, eat your heart and bury you alive, turning your head into a cobblestone.

We were power players in the biggest war Everworld had ever seen. We were four high school kids from the north shore, and a witch from who knows where. And all we had to do was find a woman who was supposed to be dead and stay alive ourselves, despite the fact that the motto in Everworld is, "When in doubt, kill 'em."

So far our major contribution to the future of this lunatic asylum was to help Vikings slaughter Aztecs, get Galahad killed, build a telegraph for the fairies, and hand gunpowder to some aliens.

And the worst of it was the terrible feeling that no matter what we did, it all helped Senna.

CHAPTER
III

The meeting was with Athena and the Coo-Hatch prisoner. It took place at Athena's home or temple — we were never sure what to call these places. Specifically, it took place in Athena's library, a cavernous room whose walls were lined with cubbyholes, each filled with one or more scrolls. It looked like the kind of place that should be as dusty as an old tomb. But there was no dust: The servants on Olympus know their stuff. I imagine they have to.

It was the five of us plus the big, gray-eyed goddess and the Coo-Hatch prisoner. There were no refreshments. A pity. I'd be interested to see how, or even if, the Coo-Hatch ate.

Coo-Hatch are odd-looking creatures. Like some nightmare flightless bird twisted into a capital letter *C*. The tips of their toes extend out about as far as the tip of their elongated funnel of a face. They have eyes that are blue within red. Kind of mesmerizing, the eyes are.

They have four arms, two obviously built for heavy lifting and two others for more delicate work. When they talk you don't see a mouth moving. When they walk they look like Groucho Marx, or maybe some comic doing a satire of a bent old man.

This Coo-Hatch was not carrying a throwing blade. The Coo-Hatch we'd first met outside the Aztec city had carried them and had demonstrated their use — a memory that kept me from ever thinking of the Coo-Hatch as harmless or humorous. On that occasion a handful of Coo-Hatch had thrown their blades and sliced a tree as easily as a deli-counter man slicing bologna.

We all stood. No chairs. Athena was not one to put you at ease. She wasn't our friend Dionysus, always offering you a glass of wine, a snack, and a blue nymph. Athena was a serious god. And this was serious business. But she had leaned her omnipresent spear against a desk the size of my garage. I guess that was her version of kicking back.

We mere mortals waited till she decided to speak. The Coo-Hatch paced back and forth, four Groucho steps, then turn, four Groucho steps back.

I wondered where the swift Tinkerbell mini Coo-Hatch was. Maybe they only traveled with the main Coo-Hatch band. We'd assumed they were juvenile Coo-Hatch, but who knew? Assumptions were dangerous when applied to aliens who had evolved in an entirely different universe.

"These devices, these instruments," Athena began, sounding uncertain. "The weapons that kill at a distance, made by the Coo-Hatch. What are they called?"

"The guns?" David suggested. "The cannon?"

"Cannon." Athena tried out the word and made a face like she found the word unsatisfactory. "Davideus, my general, you tell me that if these are made available to the Hetwan they will surely overwhelm our forces."

David didn't even blush at the "general." He'd gotten used to that pretty quickly.

"Yes, cannon, especially if the Coo-Hatch made a lot, would make it impossible to hold just about any fixed position." David added, "If you gods got into the fight, things would be different, but as long as your brother and sister gods want to rely on human soldiers, yeah, cannon will blow big holes in our lines. No way guys with swords beat guys with cannon. That's a five-minute battle."

Athena looked like she'd swallowed something she'd rather have spit out. She glared at the Coo-

Hatch, who stopped pacing and returned her gaze.

"You demand an escape from Everworld, a return to your old world? Did you think my great father, mighty Zeus, would do this for you?"

"We hoped," the Coo-Hatch said, spreading his weaker arms wide in a universal gesture of supplication. "We are desperate. Ka Anor cannot help us. We thought that Zeus, who with the other great gods created Everworld, would hold the key."

Athena shook her helmeted head. "He does not. When the great father and mother gods created Everworld they walled themselves off from the old world. Only rarely does anyone cross the great barrier. Only when an unusual mortal of great power is born." She looked at Senna. "Such a person can open a gateway, become a tunnel connecting worlds. This witch is such a mortal."

I watched Senna, looking for the arrogance, the ego that would show despite her best efforts to suppress it. She seemed small and insignificant compared to Athena.

Senna said, "I do not have the power to open a portal to the Coo-Hatch world or universe. But I may know one who does."

"So you claim," Athena said. "Your mother. Who you say is within Everworld."

"Yes. As I said before Zeus, my mother is a priestess of Isis. Her powers are greater than mine."

A lie? No evidence, nothing I could point to — I just sensed it. Senna was lying. Or at the very least concealing. But concealing what? Her own motives? Undoubtedly. But what else?

"Then you must go to her and beg for her help," Athena said, and nodded firmly. "It will be a long and perilous voyage."

"Who says we're going?" Christopher demanded peevishly, turning away from the goddess to talk to the rest of us. "I mean, come on, isn't it time for us to figure out what we're doing here? What are we, the United Nations? The One-hundred-first Air borne, rushing off to solve everyone else's problems? Did I get drunk and join the marines and no one told me?"

"We created this problem," April said. "At least some of us did." She gave me a slight nod, an acknowledgment that I had spoken out against handing our chemistry book to the Coo-Hatch to begin with. "You can't have a cannon without gunpowder, and they wouldn't have gunpowder without us."

"Boo-hoo," Christopher said. "I don't recall being asked if I wanted to come to this great big padded cell. I didn't crash the party; I was dragged here. After that point anything I have to do to keep my head attached to my neck is okay."

I said, "That's weak reasoning, Christopher. That's just the old 'I didn't ask to be born' argument. Your mom says, 'Handle your responsibilities, take out the trash,' and you say, 'I didn't ask to be born.' It's kind of childish, don't you think?"

"No, I don't," Christopher shot back. "I carry the load I agree to carry. I don't remember agreeing to save Olympus." He pretended to search his memory. "Nope. Pretty sure I'd remember if I'd said that."

"You carry the load you're born with," David said harshly. "Duty isn't just something you can ignore. Or at least, you can, but if you do you're not much of a man."

"That's *you,* David," Christopher said with a condescending laugh. "You carry the load. You love the load. Me, I'm a free man. I'll decide what load I carry. Unless," he added, thoughtful now, "unless it's a debt of . . . of honor. I mean, someone saves my life, I owe them. Yeah, but that's different."

I knew what he was thinking. We all did. Ganymede had saved Christopher's life. Christopher had failed to save Ganymede when the chance arose, and Ganymede had died a hideous death, his flesh stripped from his bones by Ka

Anor. Somehow this had affected Christopher in a way nothing else had. I didn't understand it, personally. He'd had no real chance to rescue Ganymede. David had confirmed that. Still, the changes in Christopher were not bad changes.

"We have to go," I said. I ticked the points off on my fingers, aware that this annoyed just about everyone. "One: Ka Anor is the one creating the pressure for a gateway. So no Ka Anor, no need for Senna, no need for us to be here getting dragged along in her little psychodrama. Two: We created this problem by introducing real-world technology, in this case gunpowder. Three: We have a human obligation to resist evil, and Ka Anor is evil. Even by local standards he's evil."

I saw April's eyebrows lift. "Evil? I didn't think atheists believed in evil."

"What says the witch?" Athena demanded.

Senna had looked indifferent to our posturing and debating. She shook herself slightly, like someone coming out of a daydream. "The Coo-Hatch want to escape Everworld. You need them to escape Everworld. There's only one way to accomplish this. If we fail, the Hetwan will take Olympus. With Olympus gone the rest of the gods will be taken down one by one."

I don't know what Athena saw in Senna's demeanor, her carefully bored expression. But it rang the burglar alarm in my brain. My BS detector was going off. Somehow we were once again playing into Senna's hands.

"Again, this would be in the category of 'not my problem,' all due respect to you, ma'am," Christopher said with a jerky little bow to Athena.

"Four in favor, one against. We're going," David told Athena.

Christopher threw up his hands, very theatrical, but I don't think he expected anything else. He just wanted to be able to say "I told you so" later, when we found ourselves in the middle of some horrible crap-storm.

"You must travel by land," the goddess said. "Poseidon is feuding with me and with my father. He will not allow you to travel over his waters."

"Can we take Pegasus?" David asked.

"Can we take Pegasus," Christopher muttered. "There's a question you never thought you'd hear. No, we're not trapped in loony land."

"Pegasus and his sons will not carry a witch," Athena said as casually as if she were talking about the carry-on luggage allowance for a flight to New York. "Nor will any horse. You must take chariots to pass through the Hetwan lines and go to the boundaries of our lands. After that you will travel by foot through lands that are very strange."

Christopher said, "Point of curiosity, here: Is there any part of Everworld that's not extremely warped?"

Athena did not smile. I'm pretty sure she had no sense of humor.

CHAPTER
IV

We had to take chariots to get through the Hetwan lines. So easy to say. Take the number fourteen bus. Hail a cab. Head south on the Van Ryan. Catch the purple line. Jump a chariot and ride it down Olympus.

Olympus is a mountain that stands apart from a nearly straight line of mountains of equal or larger size. What we thought of as the east face was the main stage of battle between the Greeks and the Hetwan. The battle was a sit-down war for now, a siege.

The south face of Olympus was the gentlest. It was up this face that the road serpentined into the Greek-themed amusement park the gods called home. Down toward the base of the hill, clustered beside the road, was a village, or maybe it was more than one village, I don't know. There were shops and stalls, armorers and wineshops and black-smiths and bakers and coopers and so on.

At first the Hetwan had not covered this face or blocked this road. I have a theory about the Het-wan: They are dedicated, fearless, ruthless, smart, and subtle, but not at all experienced at making war against humans. They moved in a straight line from Ka Anor's city to Olympus. They didn't understand maneuver. They didn't understand the concept of coming from an unexpected direc-tion, or even of surprise. And they didn't get the whole siege concept, not at first.

But in the last few hours they'd apparently had an intellectual breakthrough and figured out that it might be a nice idea to cut the road. Hetwan had surged forward against token Greek resis-tance, cut the road, and taken over the village.

I could see the Hetwan down there. Like ants swarming the road. Big ants that spit fire. Thou-sands of them.

Athena led us to the chariots.

The chariots were basically open wagons. They had two oversized, spoked wheels and jerked wildly back and forth and seesawed every time one of the four horses on the team tossed its head or pranced.

Five chariots. Twenty horses in all. Nickering, dancing, pawing the ground, snorting, and

dumping clods of fertilizer out on the polished
marble floor of what had to be the only five-star
horse stable ever.

Athena grinned at the sight, the excitement of
it all. She jumped into one of the chariots, giddy
as a kid on Christmas morning. She grabbed the
reins in her big hands, slipped her spear into the
handy spear-stand, and whooped a loud, wild,
half-crazy war whoop.

"I wish I could go with you!" she exulted.
"There will be dangers! There will be wild beasts
and monsters and giants and ill-disposed gods.
We would make a slaughter of it!" She shook her
helmeted head regretfully. "I often envy mortals."

It was a startling transformation, to say the
least. One minute she was the quiet, thoughtful,
confident chief executive officer or college dean.
Then, with chariots in view, she was suddenly
Robert Duvall in *Apocalypse Now* going on about
how he loved the smell of napalm in the morning.

But then, she was the goddess of war as well as
wisdom.

"Um, how do you drive one of those things?"
April wondered.

I'd been wondering the same thing. No wheel,
no pedals. No brakes as far as I could tell.

Athena actually winked at April. "Seize the reins, crack the whip, and ride with the fury of the whirlwind!" Then, in a marginally more sane voice, she added, "Also, you may want to grip this railing with your free hand."

"I'll go first," David said. But it wasn't a gung-ho statement. He was eyeing the chariots, the four spirited horses, the two rickety wheels, and, I imagine, having about the same reaction we all were having. We were talking four half-wild horses pulling an oversized skateboard downhill through creatures that were going to try to kill us.

"Got one that comes with air bags?" Christopher asked.

I climbed into my chariot. Third in line. I don't know why it was mine. The steward or whatever he was just pointed. There was a spear in the spear-stand. It was about six feet tall. The head was a foot of sharp bronze.

Standing in the chariot was a balancing act. If I shifted my weight toward the back, the front of the chariot and the tongue where the traces attached would jerk up and scare the horses. If I shifted my weight forward, the weight of the chariot was transferred directly onto the back of the horses, and they didn't like that, either.

It was like that game where you have a board balanced on a ball. Not a game I'd ever play. With my right hand I grabbed the reins the way the steward showed me. In theory I could manipulate the reins and direct each horse separately. Not happening. I bunched the leather thongs in my fist and decided to just hold on. My left hand gripped the ornate, waist-high side of the chariot.

David was in chariot number one. Senna behind him. Then me, April, and Christopher.

April, sounding almost as nervous as I felt, chattered, "Guess we'd get some looks pulling up to the Burger King drive through, huh?"

"Go with the blessings of all Olympus!" Athena cried suddenly. "Go, go, heroes of Athena!"

Suddenly the doors of the stables swung open. Blue sky, marble street, massive Greek columned buildings.

David's team exploded. Senna next, but I wasn't watching them any longer, I was holding on, scrabbling, on my knees on the floor of the chariot, trying to pull myself back up with my left hand, pulling on the reins. A violent jerk, and I slammed face-first into the chariot wall, my teeth bit lip and I tasted my own blood.

I yelled a curse and pulled myself up to a standing position — if by standing you mean half-kneeling, trembling, and hanging on with a death grip.

Chaos. That's what I saw. David somewhere

out front, Senna more or less beside me, looking, I was pleased to see, about as rough as I did. I didn't have the nerve to look behind me. I was supposed to be driving this absurd, murderous device. Right.

To say that I was not exactly in control is like saying that a man hanging by his fingernails from the top floor of the Sears Tower during a hurricane is not exactly in control. The horses had decided this was a race. My horses, all white, were trying to catch David's all-black team and edge out Senna's brown animals.

The race was straight down the main drag of Olympus. I caught fractured images of people leaping out of the way. Of gods watching with interest and appreciation. I had the sense that bets were being made. Probably betting on whether I'd fall off and do a *Ben-Hur* under the wheels of whoever was behind me.

We were running on marble. I don't know how the horse's hooves even got a grip. But the wheels didn't. The entire chariot swung wildly, sliding left and right as much as five feet.

Then suddenly we were out of Olympus and charging almost straight downward. That's how it felt and how it looked. Gravity was pulling us now and the horse's feet were blurs, clattering blurs, racing to accelerate toward the center of

the earth. Faster, faster. The chariot no longer
skidded; now it vibrated. Vibrated like my teeth
were going to be broken and come tinkling out of
my mouth.

People managed to fight from these things?
How?

Down, down the narrowing road, down and
around a curve so sharp that my right wheel went
over the side. I was in a Wile E. Coyote moment,
half my chariot hanging out over a sheer drop.
Then, wham, and my knees buckled and we were
back on the road.

"Slow the hell down!" I screamed at the horses,
which, of course, interpreted this as, "Faster! Faster!"

The reins had squeezed all the blood out of my
fingers, which had gone numb and buzzy. I tried
hauling back on the reins. I mean, I've seen old
Westerns. That's what you do, you haul back on
the reins and yell, "Whoa!"

I hauled, the horses yanked back, and I nearly
lost my arm from the elbow down. This wasn't
about us, the pathetic humans, riding in our little
baskets. This was twenty stallions in a fever of
competition, fighting among themselves to see
which one could kill its passengers first.

Down and down. Not normal. Any ordinary
horse would be tired. Any ordinary animal would
slow down now. A curve! Oh —

Airborne! My entire chariot hung in the air, wheels spinning. I floated up, feet in the air, holding on with one hand, wrist twisted in the reins. Then a slamming hit that seemed designed to yank my spine right out of my body.

I hauled myself erect again. I was going to die. This was impossible. Athena. All her fault. Goddess of wisdom, my butt. This was like giving a toddler a Ferrari and a full tank of gas.

And now, Hetwan. Ahead, on the road, a dozen or more and many more rushing up to block the way. Some were buckling on the cones we called SuperSoakers. The SuperSoakers fired flaming goo, like napalm spitwads that burned into your skin.

I saw David's horses hit the first row of Hetwan. I saw a Hetwan come out from under his wheels, crumpled, to become a speed bump for the rest of us.

Then I hit the Hetwan wall. Flaming meteorites flew. One of the horses was hit, and now it was sheer madness. The horse shrieked in pain and panicked. It was rearing and kicking and throwing its head wildly while the other three horses kept going doggedly, dragging their companion along.

Then a second horse was hit. The panic became infectious.

The chariot was a rag doll in the mouth of a

mad dog. I let go of the reins and gripped the railing with both hands, tried to wedge my legs in, sank to the floor of the chariot, pain with every bump. It was like being locked inside the clothes dryer. I didn't know up or down or left or right; all I knew was that I was being beaten bloody with my own chariot.

A shooting pain, sheer agony, fire burning a neat round hole in my side, just below the armpit, no way to reach it, agony. Agony.

I didn't feel the knock that put me under — I was just suddenly in the hallway between classes, on my way to calc and nervously looking forward to seeing Miyuki, when I fell back against a locker, dropped my books, and yelled a certain four-letter word that honor students don't yell in the hallway, especially five feet away from a knot of three teachers.

For about five seconds I just stood there, panting, staring. And the three of them gaped at me, expressions of surprise dissolving into identical expressions of disapproval and outrage.

"Mr. Sherman!" one of them snapped.

CHAPTER V

But I was back across, leaving my poor real-world self to apologize to the teachers, while Everworld me came around, groggy, bumping along on the floor of the chariot, fingernails dug into a crack between boards.

I repeated the word, hauled myself up yet again, and only slowly realized that the chariot had slowed down. The horses were all behaving more or less normally. No Hetwan. I looked back; the Hetwan were way back up the hill. We were past them, past the village, off the mountain. Five chariots pulled by panting, foaming at the mouth, but seemingly happy horses.

Too long, I thought. I was only back in the real world for a moment. But I had to have been unconscious for at least five minutes. What happened to the time? I understood that Everworld time and real-world time moved differently. But wasn't something missing? Was there a sort of "travel time" between universes?

"That's good, Jalil," I muttered under my breath. "Worry about the travel time. Makes perfect sense."

The road was down on more or less level ground now. Pleasant country of vineyards and cultivated patches of ground defined by neat piled-rock walls.

I took inventory. Bloody lip. Bruises on every square inch of my body. A deep, nasty burn in my side. I expected to be able to see a rib through the burn hole.

"Everyone okay?" David yelled back in a loud but shaky voice.

"Yeah, David, I'm fine!" Christopher yelled. "Never better. Hey, I know what we can do next: Let's just cram ourselves into a damn Cuisinart and hit 'puree.' Am I okay? Freaking great, David. Time of my life. Cool party. Let's do it all over again, only this time let's get some big guys to beat on us with baseball bats, because this is just so much fun."

Senna was beside me, just a bit ahead. Her face was bloody, but nothing gushing. Strands of hair were plastered down across her face. I saw she was favoring her right arm.

Not that I was happy she was hurt. But this was

all her fault, after all, and damned if I'd have wanted to see her all smug and well-groomed. I was not in a generous or forgiving mood.

I twisted around, as well as I could with the breath-stopping pain in my side and the stiffness that came from rigid terror. I looked at April. Her red hair was wild. Her green eyes were wild. She looked a bit like a person who has just been hit by lightning. But other than that she looked okay. Not happy, but okay.

"Let's get out and walk," Christopher shouted from the back. "Who knows when these crazy-assed horses will decide to freak again?"

At which point a voice said, "We have orders from gray-eyed Athena herself to carry you safely to the borders of this land."

Silence from the five of us. Then April said, "Who said that?"

"That would be one of my horses," David said, trying to sound unamazed.

"The horses talk," I said. "Of course they talk. Why wouldn't they talk? Excuse me, boys," I said to my own horses. "Didn't you hear me begging you to slow down back there?"

"Jalil, man, you talking to horses?" Christopher mocked. The road had widened and we were more nearly abreast.

"Yes, I am, Christopher. I am talking to horses. And here's what's sad: I'm a little pissed that they won't answer."

"W.T.E., man." Welcome To Everworld.

"It's not much farther now," one of my horses said, evidently taking pity on me.

Christopher laughed. And then, so did I.

It was all impossible, of course. All of it. But I guess at some point there's not much you can do besides laugh.

And yet, even as we all began to laugh, even to giggle, the nervous reaction to having been scared to death, my mind was wondering: *Where was my mind when it was neither here nor there? What was "between" Everworld and the real world? And why did time elapse en route?*

It was another hour at a mellow pace, sometimes a walk, sometimes a trot, before the horses announced that we were there.

I didn't notice a "there." But what was I going to do? Argue with a horse?

"I'm taking the spear," Christopher said. I thought that was a good idea. We all did, all but Senna. I guess carrying a weapon would have been a sign of weakness in her mind. Her weapon was her magic.

We climbed down on shaky legs. The chariots turned and the horses headed toward Olympus like factory workers punching out of work. They looked like they might stop off somewhere and catch a few beers before heading on home.

The mountains loomed huge behind us, running away to what seemed to be our southeast. Olympus dominated the landscape, a sheer-sided mountain with a top poked up into the clouds.

From here we couldn't see the temples, the marble street, or the Hetwan army. I felt odd. Nostalgic. Homesick. Like I wanted to be back there and couldn't be.

April must have seen me gazing back longingly.

"They have great food," she commented. "Great room service."

"Yeah. May be a long time before we see clean clothes and clean sheets again."

"Weird, huh? It seems like home, kind of. Like that little house is ours. I guess you have to find a place to call home, even if you know it's nonsense."

I smiled. "You're starting to fit in here, April. You're becoming an Everworlder."

I meant it as a compliment, or at least as a gentle tease.

But April's eyes went wide, then narrowed severely. She bit her lip like I'd called her a name and stalked off along the road.

CHAPTER
VI

We walked along a road that became less of a
road with each step. What had begun on Olympus as a wide, marble-paved avenue was now just
dried mud. The mud must have been deep fairly
recently, and it had been churned by countless
hooves. Probably cows, though in Everworld it
might just as easily have been a herd of unicorns.

We topped a low ridge and looked out over a
landscape startlingly different from the one we'd
left behind. Look back to olive groves and vineyards. Look ahead to knee-high grass the color of
Christopher's hair, and scattered, lonely trees
that looked as if they'd been allowed to grow to
some regulation height then smeared horizontal
by a passing celestial butter knife.

Look back on a well-watered land, fluffy clouds,
streams, black-speckled white boulders erupting

from a lush but unmowed lawn. Look ahead to a place that hinted at nearby deserts. A dry, hot wind blew in your face.

"I'll say one thing for Everworld," Christopher said. "It doesn't take long to get from one place to the next."

"This is just ridiculous," I said. "Climate cannot change this quickly. It can't be temperate one minute and semi-arid the next. You cannot have temperatures ten or twenty degrees different between your front and your back. Impossible."

"Yeah, well, I guess no one told the gods that," David remarked.

"It's like a big quilt," April muttered, still annoyed at me for some reason, but trying to be civil.

Her analogy was perfect. I was surprised. Not by the fact that she was right, but by the fact I had not thought of that example yet. "Exactly. It's a big quilt. That's exactly right. Each god designed his own piece and then they sewed it together without worrying too much about an overall picture. The weather patterns, the vegetation, the land features, they all stay within the patch."

"There's some crossover," David pointed out. "Animals, people. Various types of people."

"Yes," I agreed, "and plants as well, but they're

less adaptable to differing climates. Especially at borders like this where you have radically different patches. If you have a cold deciduous forest alongside a cold evergreen forest, you'll have crossover. But up ahead here we have savanna, and behind us we have grapevines. The grapes are not going to grow up ahead there."

"Deciduous?" Christopher echoed. "What's the deal with you, Jalil? Did you actually pay attention in, like, sixth grade? Hey, does anyone see any gymnosperms?"

"Do you actually know what a gymnosperm is?" I asked.

"The diagnosis for a guy named Jim who can't have kids?" Christopher asked innocently, then began to cackle like an idiot at his own joke. "I have been saving that since junior high. Years I have waited to use that joke. What a relief."

"Glad I could help," I muttered, determined not to crack a smile despite the fact both David and April were grinning, enjoying Christopher's obvious relish of his own lame joke.

"There's something moving up ahead," Senna said.

A dark, sinuous movement across the grass, far off. It might almost be heat shimmer. Then the herd turned and came toward us. Deer. Antelope. But strange in shape. They had horns that flared off to the sides, like very bad toupees, and humps.

"Wildebeests?" April wondered.

"I don't know if they will, you'll have to ask them," Christopher muttered, but this time did not even find his own joke funny.

"Think this is the right way?" David asked Senna.

She shrugged. "One minute we're in Greece, now I guess we're in sub-Saharan Africa. Normally I'd say we must have missed Egypt, but who knows? This is where Athena sent us. This may be the way."

"Or not," I said.

David shook his head, not sure, but started walking just the same, down the slope of the ridge, leaving all evidence of a gentler Mediterranean climate behind us.

David fell into step beside me. He was the only one not using his spear as a walking stick. He carried it leaned back on his shoulder, like a soldier carrying a rifle. "Jalil, what do you know about the gods and so on in Africa?"

"Well, Bwana, about as much as you do."

"Hey, I wasn't asking because you're black, I was asking because you're . . . because you know stuff I don't."

"Uh-huh."

"Look, it's not a diss to think maybe someone knows something about his own heritage," David argued, shifting position.

"You know much about the kings of ancient Israel? I mean, what was the deal with Habakkuk anyway? How about Solomon's temple?"

"I hear it's very tastefully decorated," Christopher interjected.

"Point made," David conceded.

"Here's what I know about ancient Africa: It's not a place. It's not 'black folk.' It's hundreds, maybe thousands of different nationalities. All kinds of different languages — of course, in Everworld even the horses speak English, so I'm guessing you won't need to worry about that. But you've got all kinds of different beliefs. You've got your cattle ranchers and your farmers and your warriors and your live-and-let-live hippies and your crazy jungle head-hunters. There are some big-time, Roman-style empires with tens of thousands of warriors and gold everywhere, and there are little bands of primitive people walking around with Frisbees stuck in their lips. Just saying 'Africa' is like saying 'Europe.' You know? A Frenchman living in Paris in the court of some King Louis the Whatever can't just be lumped in with some frozen, bearskin-wearing, reindeer-eating Popsicle up in Lapland."

"Kind of touchy, isn't he?" Christopher said.

"Never ask him something where he doesn't know the answer. Jalil is incapable of just saying, 'I don't know.' You ask him something he doesn't know, and he'll go on twice as long."

I shot a dirty look at Christopher, but truth was, he had me and he knew it, and I knew it.

"Here's a question," Christopher said. "Tarzan. Is he a myth? And if he is, are we going to run into him?"

"Lions," Senna said.

It took me a second to figure out what she meant. It sounded like she was answering Christopher. Then I saw them. Lions. A pride, maybe a dozen lions, counting the juveniles, all lounging in the shade of a cluster of trees. A lioness was sitting, head up, watching the wildebeests, but the rest were on their backs or sides, snoring away the morning.

"We're downwind," David said. "Better make sure we stay downwind. Let's cut left here, give them a wide berth."

"Surely you're not afraid of lions, Davideus," Senna taunted.

"They're bigger than I am, faster, stronger, and on their own turf," David said evenly.

"I'm with you there," I agreed.

We cut left, which meant leaving the wandering suggestion of a road and setting out into the grass. The road hadn't been much but it was easier than walking through the grass, which dragged at our steps and slowed us down. And hidden by the grass were ruts and burrow holes that were practically designed for twisting an ankle. We kept the breeze against our right cheeks and moved at an angle to the pride. Only when we were well past them did we at last turn back to our original heading.

But now the grass was taller, reaching to our waists. And vast expanses of vicious thornbushes crowded us first from one side, then the other. Casual conversation petered out as we all began to feel a bit hemmed in, a bit trapped. We couldn't see the lion pride anymore; the view was blocked by the dry, brown thornbushes. A thicket I was confident the lions could glide through unscathed to ambush us.

Then, a shock of adrenaline. A man. Standing where I had looked just a moment before. As if he'd appeared out of thin air, or at the very least stepped from the thorns.

He was black, dressed in a simple loincloth. He had a skin pouch hanging from a belt. He was old, thin, a walking piece of beef jerky. His hair was white, cut tall so that it seemed to extend in a tapered cone up and back from his head. The hair added a foot and a half to his height.

"Yah!" Christopher yelped, noticing him a moment later. "It's Don King! It's Don King half naked."

David motioned us to stop. The five of us stood there, midstream in a river of grass that passed between banks of thornbushes.

David said, "I don't see a weapon. And he looks human."

Christopher caught my eye and, deliberately provoking, said, "Jalil, why don't you talk to him, man? Ask him what he wants. I'll take the next reindeer-eating Laplander we meet."

The man in the loincloth stared at us for a while, expressionless. Then, the sudden flash of a smile and a wave of his hand.

"Maybe he could tell us where we are," April suggested.

"Ask him if he's seen any pyramids around here," Senna said dryly.

I refused to speak to the old man. I wasn't playing this game. This was not my personal responsibility just because this old man and I shared pigmentation.

David waited, realized I was leaving it to him, and finally yelled, "Hi!"

No answer. Just the smile.

"Um, what's this country called?" David shouted.

The old man laughed. He seemed to find that a pretty good joke.

"Okay," David muttered under his breath. Then in a friendly yell, "Excuse me, sir, I know this sounds fairly crazy, but we're looking for Egypt."

"Like getting off the plane at O'Hare and asking someone 'Which way to Montana?'" April said.

"Maybe he knows," David said defensively.

"Do you speak?" Senna demanded, obviously impatient. "What's your name, old man?"

The old man stopped smiling. He stared at her. Right at her. He had bright, active eyes. *Shrewd eyes*, I thought.

"Eshu," the man said at last. "I am called Eshu."

"Gesundheit." Christopher, of course.

The old man smiled as if he got the joke. "Where are you going?" he inquired politely.

"Egypt," David answered for us. "Do you know the fastest way through all this?"

"Be careful when you travel. Don't rush and neglect your duty," Eshu said. "Sacrifices must be made, respects must be paid."

"Yep, and a penny saved is a penny earned and a stitch in time saves nine." I don't know why I was snappish. Normally I'd at least have been polite. But the old man seemed to be addressing each of his remarks to me specifically now, and I didn't want to be singled out. Eshu and I shared a skin color, that was all. If I resented the others treating me like the appointed Africa expert, I didn't like it any better coming from a fortune-cookie-spouting character in a loincloth.

"Mortal man must pay respect," Eshu said.

"Respect this," Christopher said as we saddled up again to move away from the old man.

"The lions come," Eshu said.

"What? What did he say?"

A blur. Just a blur, close to the ground, a cannonball fired at grass level, a flash in my brain, a single image composed of hurtling speed and irresistible power.

I opened my mouth to yell, but the lioness was on me before I could breathe.

CHAPTER
VII

Conscious. Aware. Eyes open.

On my back.

I was on my back in the grass and it was night with more stars than I'd ever seen before, hard white diamonds strewn across a black sky. On my back, with a fire nearby, not close enough to warm me, and I was so cold.

Wrong. Everything was wrong.

Something was tugging on me, pulling at me, yanking me. I raised my head with difficulty and looked down. The lion had hold of one of my organs and was trying to rip it free, worrying it, tugging at it, trying to snap the cord of viscera that held it attached to me.

I was hollowed out. I saw it in the flicker of firelight. Saw white ribs. Mine. Saw a concavity, a raw, bloody mess where my stomach had been.

The lions were all around me. The big, full-maned males were gnawing on my flesh, bits of me torn loose and dragged through the dirt. The lionesses gnawed at what was left. At my legs. They stripped the flesh off my thighs, like someone eating a piece of chicken. One of them tore a long, quivering, dark red muscle, ripped it clear off with one big yank of her head.

I was dead. Had to be. No pain. Where was the pain? I felt it, felt the teeth, felt the pull and tug, felt the shock of cold on bones that had never been exposed to air.

Hyenas cavorted just at the edge of the circle of light. Waiting their turn. That was the way, wasn't it? The lions ate what they wanted, then came the hyenas to use their massive jaws to crack open bones and shatter my skull and eat the marrow within. And finally the vultures.

A dream? Too real. Too real. Ah, ah, ah, ah, ah! NO. No, no, nonononononono. No. No. No. They were eating me. I was still alive and they were eating me, eating me, ripping me apart, tearing out my insides.

Panic. Fight it. Why? Why? I was dead, I could panic if I wanted to.

Only I wasn't dead. I was seeing, hearing, feeling, smelling the foulness as a lion tore open my intestines and spilled the mess.

Not dead. Alive. Not possible. No, think, Jalil. This couldn't be real. Couldn't be.

Why? Why couldn't it be real? This wasn't the real world, this was Everworld — what couldn't be real here in this place? What was outlawed here? A man watching his own body being ripped apart like a slab of baby back ribs? Yes, why not? It was real. It was real. Help me! Someone help me!

No. Fight it, Jalil. Fight it. Fight it. Fightfightfightfightfight. Not real. An illusion. Why, Jalil? What's your proof? What makes this unreal? Why is it a trick, please, please prove it, Jalil. Prove it's a lie.

You've seen similar things, Jalil, you remember: the men in Hel's grip. Dead but alive. Alive in eternal torment. If that was real, why isn't this? Why is the lion's hot breath on your face, the sight of it, so huge, gazing down at you with liquid gold eyes, why is it not real, why is it not real that it's oh, no no no, eating your face, Jalil, sinking its teeth into your face, your cheeks, tearing, ripping, crushing, crushing till your brain . . .

Brain. Brain, that's why. That's why. Everworld may be Everworld, but I am me. I am Jalil. I am this brain in this head on this body, and my rules are the rules of the real world.

There's no thought without brain, no mind without brain. That's why it's a lie. Because my brain is seeping like warm oatmeal through the crack in my skull.

And that can't be. That's me, that's Jalil, that oat-meal, that mush cramped inside an airless, lightless cave of bone, that's me.

"It's not a dream," I said, speaking with half a tongue and a jaw that was no longer completely attached to my head. "If it was a dream I'd be in the real world. I'm still in Everworld. I'm not asleep. I'm conscious. And this is an illusion."

The lion stopped eating my face. It spoke. "Not real? What *is* real, Jalil?"

"You're not real," I said firmly.

"And yet, you speak to me. In denying me you make me real. Real to you, which is all the reality there will ever be."

I felt around with my right hand. I seemed to still have a right hand. I pushed it into my pocket and touched my knife. I drew it slowly out and with trembling, numb fingers I snapped open the blade of Coo-Hatch steel.

"This blade will cut anything real," I said. "Will you bleed?"

I slashed. My knife went through air. The lion was gone.

My eyes snapped open. Bright sunlight. I slapped my hand on my belly and felt my own skinny self. All of me.

I sat up.

"Hey, hey, take it easy with that knife," April

said. She was sitting beside me. She pressed me back down, hand against my chest. "Take five minutes, okay? You just scared the hell out of us."

"What happened?" I demanded, sweating, shaky.

"A lion attacked you. Knocked you down. We think your head hit that rock there."

"It didn't eat me?" I demanded, not caring very much if I sounded insane.

"No, thanks to Eshu," April said. "He used some kind of sling. He hit the lion with a rock."

I pushed April away, firmly but not rudely, and sat up. The old African with the Don King hair squatted nearby, seemingly indifferent. He was looking off toward the horizon.

"A rock?" I demanded. "You all have spears, and David has his sword."

"Hey, sorry," David said peevishly, "but it's not all that easy to hit a moving lioness with a spear and not skewer your ingrate of a friend in the process."

No. He was right, of course. "Sorry," I said. "Thanks for not skewering me."

"It's Eshu you should thank," April insisted.

"A rock, huh?" I said. The lions that had killed and eaten me had only been real in my imagination. But that was enough to know one thing: A lion doesn't run from a rock.

I glanced at Senna. She was staring daggers at Eshu, who remained the picture of nonchalance.

Then Eshu turned his face toward me, just for a second, unobserved by anyone but Senna and me. Eshu looked at me and grinned an amused and malicious grin.

I don't know why I didn't say anything to the others right then. Maybe because anything I said would have sounded paranoid. They'd have thought I suffered a concussion. They'd seen what they'd seen, and what I'd been through would be easily dismissed as a nightmare, the obvious result of a concussion combined with terror.

But there was another reason to keep quiet. Whoever, whatever this Eshu was, he'd messed with my mind in a powerful way. I felt abused. I felt wronged. But I also felt like I'd won a skirmish in a larger battle. Magic versus Reason, and Reason had won. Maybe I couldn't make all of Everworld bow to the rules I knew to be true, but I could take this one guy.

Chapter VIII

We were crossing the African savanna, there was no denying that fact. It was Africa, or a part of it, anyway. But an Africa that existed long before the advent of safaris of well-heeled suburbanites crammed into Land Rovers for a look at wild animals.

This was Africa before slave traders and colonialists and corrupt governments. Whichever gods had stolen this land and carried it away to Everworld had, I assume, meant it to stay this way forever.

We were out of the thorns, back onto the sea of yellow grass. We passed not far from a village of mud and thatch huts that baked in the relentless sun, a grim little pimple on the savanna.

But an hour later we passed another village, more sophisticated, larger, a town actually, surrounded by well-tended fields irrigated by a complex system of ditches and canals. I could see a marketplace filled with men and women and various animals, cattle, goats, and pigs. The town had low adobe walls guarded by large warriors dressed in zebra skins and carrying tall shields and long spears.

Clearly the two villages were very different peoples. One more anomaly. One more thing that made no sense

Eshu led us around both the miserable village and the prosperous town. The guards watched us pass and did not challenge us. Eshu gave them a casual wave, as though they were acquaintances.

Eshu had become our guide. I wasn't in a position to object. After all, hadn't he scared off the lion that tried to kill me? What was I going to say? He's a witch doctor of some sort? Christopher would have ridden me for a week over that.

So I trudged along behind the old man, keeping pace with the others. I bided my time, steeled for the next, inevitable confrontation. I was almost anxious for it. I'd taken the nightmare and overcome it. I was high off the win.

We were spread out over twenty yards or so. I noticed that Senna always kept the maximum distance between herself and Eshu.

I dropped back to pace her. And when I was

sure no one else would overhear, I said, "So what is he?"

Senna gave me an appraising look. Her first impulse was to blow me off, I think, but then it occurred to her that she and I were the only two who knew something was wrong. I was her potential ally.

"I don't know," she admitted.

"A god?"

She shook her head doubtfully. "I don't know. I don't think so. Something else, maybe. What did he do to you?"

"You don't know?" I was a little surprised.

"I know he did something. I could feel it. He'd wrapped you up in some kind of field, some kind of . . . I don't know what to call it. I felt his powers, that's all. I felt they were centered on you."

I sucked in a deep breath scented with rich soil and fresh-mown hay. "Let me ask you this: Are you scared of him or is he scared of you?"

A faint, ironic smile. "Right to the point. That's why I like you, Jalil. You always know the right question."

"And you always know how to avoid answering."

"The Coo-Hatch are following us."

"What?" I turned around to look.

"You can't see them now. There's a small band

of them. I spotted one of the juveniles flying behind us, keeping just within visual range."

I felt a crawly sensation on the back of my neck. "Keeping tabs on us? Making sure we do what we said we'd do."

"Don't ask me to explain Coo-Hatch. I don't understand them any better than you do."

"Maybe they're annoyed at you for having murdered one of them," I said.

Senna looked straight ahead. The steel door rattled down, sealing her off. Conversation over. I quickened my pace a little to catch up to David, who was up ahead with Eshu.

"Senna says there are Coo-Hatch following us."

David nodded. "Yeah. I know. I don't think it's a problem."

"Might be nice for you to keep us lesser folk informed, General."

He looked surprised. "Sorry. You're right."

Hard to be mad at someone who apologizes. Which was too bad because I wanted to be mad at someone, anyone besides Eshu. Being mad at him gave him power over me.

"Why aren't we stopping at any of these villages?" I asked David. "We could use some water."

He jerked his head toward Eshu. "Our guide says these aren't good places to get a drink. He says we'll find wells ahead."

So we walked. The waterskins Athena had given us were nearly empty, and the sun was blazingly hot, relentless. There was no shade and no one had sunglasses. I felt like I'd go blind if I didn't find some shade soon, someplace where I could close my eyes.

At one point a herd of zebra half sauntered, half trotted across our path, uninterested in us. I saw some sort of gazelle or antelope, more zebra, and a pair of far-distant elephants.

I was more interested in the two or three dozen trees that seemed to be right in our path. I watched those trees and their cool shade. I wanted to stop there, hoped we would, but was determined not to ask Eshu for anything.

At last we reached the trees. The shade was not cool, but it was shade. And there was a well, a circle of mud bricks and a leather skin hanging from a dipping arm.

"This is good water," Eshu said.

"After you," David said, ushering the old man forward. It might have been mere politeness, but I'm sure David was using Eshu to test the water first.

The old man grinned, shook his head at some private joke, and drew himself a skin full of water. He drank deep, paused, drank again.

"Good enough," Christopher muttered. "Although I'd sell whatever's left of my soul for a cold beer."

We drank, and we sat under the trees and ate some of what we'd brought from Olympus. April's face was bright red, sunburned. And freckles had appeared.

"I never noticed you have freckles," Christopher said.

"I don't. Usually. It's this sun." She touched her forehead and nose gingerly.

I said, "We need to get you a hat, April."

Eshu stared at April with interest. "The sun burns your face."

"Yes, I'm afraid we redheads were not meant for the African sun."

"Maybe the sun would not burn so bright if you asked it to hide its face," Eshu suggested.

"Asked it?" April echoed, amused. "That's all I have to do, ask it?"

Eshu shrugged his spindly shoulders. "You would need to offer a sacrifice, of course."

"What? What do you mean?"

Eshu pointed. "One of those baboons would do."

There was a troop of baboons. Clearly visible and audible — I could hear them gibbering and screeching — a hundred yards away across the little oasis. They had not been there before. I'd have noticed. I was confident I'd have noticed. I shot a look at David. Yes, he was as surprised as I was. His eyes narrowed suspiciously.

Good. Eshu was outing himself.

"You want me to sacrifice a baboon?" April asked, more amused than anything. "Gee, I don't think so."

Eshu shrugged. "It is your choice."

The conversation moved on, then faltered. We were tired, sleepy from the sun, and getting dopey. I guess there's a reason they have *siesta* time in tropical climes without air-conditioning.

I noticed April already asleep, slumped on her side, eyes fluttering like she was having a dream.

Eshu rocked slowly, back and forth, back and forth, silent.

All at once I knew. Senna? Yes, she was staring hard at the old man. Yes, he was doing it. To April this time.

I got up, stepped over to April, and shook her shoulder roughly. "Wake up."

She woke screaming. Screaming and screaming and pawing at her face.

"What the —" David yelled, leaped up, and yanked his sword out.

"Damn, April!" Christopher cried. "You scared the pee out of me."

April was calming, but only slowly. She was

touching her face, her arms, looking at her arms and legs, pulling up her shirt to look at her belly. There were tears in her eyes. A haunted look on her face.

"Nightmare," she whispered, almost to herself.

"Did it involve me?" Christopher asked innocently, then laughed lewdly. "Because sometimes you show up in my dreams, April. If you see where I'm going with that."

April tried to shake off the horrible, lingering memory of the dream that was no dream. She even tried to counter Christopher. "If it had been about you, Christopher, I'd have . . ." She lost track of what she was saying and looked hard at Eshu.

"Who the hell are you?" she snapped. It's rare to hear April curse. It got everyone's attention.

"I am Eshu."

"Yeah? That's your name. What are you?"

He seemed nonplussed, but it was fake. He was suppressing a mischievous grin. "I am as you see."

"You have a job, Eshu?" Christopher asked.

"Ah. Yes. I am a messenger."

"What, African Express?"

Eshu spread his hands, a humble gesture. "I am a simple messenger. Someone has a message to send, and I carry it where it should go."

I said, "What message are you carrying now?"

Eshu looked at his hands, turned them over, and again. "My hands are empty."

"Get rid of him," Senna said.

"Why?" David demanded.

"He has powers," she said simply.

"I will humbly take my leave," Eshu said with a sort of courtly bow. "To reach your goal, merely keep going in this same direction. But you must also be prepared to make necessary sacrifices."

"Is that a threat?" David snapped.

Eshu smiled, almost gentle. "It is a message."

The old man turned and walked away. He looked harmless and even a bit forlorn.

"Okay, let's get moving again," David said. No one objected.

April was still running her fingers over her face. Still searching for the burn that wasn't there.

CHAPTER IX

I walked beside April. "Hey, take your back-pack, crumple it up, pull the straps down and tie them together. You'll have a kind of hat. You can carry the stuff in your shirt."

She tried it. It took a few tries but it worked. "Thanks."

"No problem. I wish I'd thought of it earlier. So. Tell me about it."

"Tell you about what?"

"You know what. Tell me yours, I'll tell you mine."

It had not occurred to her that I'd had a similar "nightmare." She was surprised.

"The sun," she said. "I was being burned alive by the sun. My skin was bubbling up, like chicken skin in a hot oven. Peeling off. Tattered bits of skin actually catching fire. Hair burned off. Eyebrows. My eyes themselves . . . like boiled eggs. It was incredibly vivid. It felt absolutely real."

I related my own nightmare.

"You think it's Eshu?" she asked.

"Don't you? Anyway, Senna thinks it's him. You heard her. I think she has the witch version of 'gaydar.' She can sense someone like herself."

"Well, anyway, he's gone," April said.

I scanned the horizon. No sign of the old man. The elephants were closer. And now there were round-shouldered mountains in sight, startling, deep green, rising abruptly from the grass. They were a long way off still, but the suddenness of the shift from savanna to lush, jungle-clothed hills was disturbing.

We walked for two more hours before we spotted a place to rest again. Fewer trees this time, but they were beside a stream that ran swiftly down from the looming green hills. This time we saw the baboon colony right from the start. They were downstream, which was probably a good thing. We didn't want to try and drink water the baboons had used.

"You think they have germs here in Everworld?" Christopher wondered as he knelt to scoop up mouthfuls of water.

"That's a good question," I said. "It's a very interesting question. I wonder. I don't know whether the gods brought actual, literal chunks of the old world with them, and thus could be expected to have imported bacteria and viruses and other microscopic life along. Or whether everything here is a product of a sort of ill-informed Xeroxing. But you know —"

"Remind me not to come up with any other good questions," Christopher interrupted. "The water tastes okay. I guess if I get the creeping African cruds, we'll know they have germs in Everworld."

"We may have imported germs ourselves," I said. "We could end up being devastating disease vectors, you know, like when the Europeans brought smallpox to the New World and killed hundreds of thousands of Indians who didn't have natural immunities."

"Here's a question for you," Christopher said. "How come it's only the white man who brought diseases to America? Everyone's always talking about the white man bringing smallpox and whatever. Black folk didn't bring diseases? I mean, come on. Africa has diseases the rest of the world doesn't even want to think about."

"Christopher," April warned.

"No, it's a good question," I said, a little alarmed that Christopher was suddenly causing me to think.

He gave himself a congratulatory flourish. "Thank you, thank you very much."

"Hey." David. "Hey, you guys? April? April, come over here."

He sounded agitated. He was upstream a few dozen yards. The three of us trotted up to meet him. He was staring uncertainly at a small girl dressed in a crude shift.

"Huh," I said. Not a brilliant remark.

"It's a little girl," Christopher said.

David turned a nervous face to April. "April?"

April rolled her eyes at David and laughed. Then she knelt down by the girl, who stood with toes in, belly stuck out, and thumb in her mouth. I guessed she was maybe five or six years old.

"Hi. Hi there. My name is April, what's your name?"

"Think she speaks English?" David wondered.

I said, "David, for some reason everyone here speaks English, including dragons, pigs, and flying horses. Or at least we understand it as English."

"Good point."

"Don't be scared, honey," April said in her best soothing voice. "Can you tell me your name?"

"My name is Elegbara," the little girl said.

"Elegbara? That's a beautiful name," April cooed. "Where are your mommy and daddy?"

Elegbara looked confused. Then she pointed. The same direction we were traveling. "Bad spirits came and they ran away. Our village is that way."

"Bad spirits?" David echoed, going into military mode. He began searching the horizon.

"What's that, like they got depressed? Bad spirits?" Christopher wondered.

"Around here I'd go for the more literal interpretation," I muttered.

"So would I," Christopher said. "I was just trying to cling to hope for a minute longer."

"What are these bad spirits like?" David asked the girl.

"Bad spirits, evil ones," she said with a shrug, like he was asking which way was up.

"Why were they going after your folks?"

The little girl looked thoughtful and bit her lip. "My grandmother says everyone must make sacrifices to show respect for the great high gods and the Orisha. If proper sacrifices are not made, if respect is not shown, trouble follows."

"That's some speech for a little kid," I said. "And I'm hearing the word 'sacrifice' a little too often. Senna!"

Senna was off by herself, as she generally was. In this case she was watching the baboons with interest. She had not seen the little girl. In response to my yell she sauntered our way, playing with a twist of grass.

She stopped dead when she saw the little girl, and the girl began to laugh gleefully. The laughter went from little-girl falsetto to old man's rasp. Elegbara became Eshu.

David cursed and drew his sword. "I wanted to give you the benefit of the doubt, but you know what? You've stepped over the line. You walk away and live, or you stay and I'll take your head right off your shoulders."

Eshu laughed and clapped his hands in delight. "Oh, please do not harm me, great warrior."

"Get away from us and stay away from us," David ordered.

Eshu stopped laughing. "You come into Eshu's land and order Eshu to leave?"

"That's exactly right," David said tersely.

Eshu smiled a steely smile. "Eshu will go. But the sacrifices will be made. Respects will be paid. This is not your land, but ours."

He turned and walked away, transforming himself as he went, back into the little girl.

"He's no Loki, but he's a pain in the ass just the same," Christopher said.

"Sacrifice. That's the key word here," I said. "Like I said, I'm hearing that word a lot. He wants something from us. He wants us to —"

A scream. Inhuman. Above!

The tree above us was full of them! Dark, glowing skeletons, fangs dripping blood, long claws for hands.

And all at once they were falling, dropping from the trees, swarming down on us.

My spear. Where was it, where had I left it? Two of the creatures — shrieking, gloating demons — were tearing at me with their fingers. I punched and kicked. The blows landed, meant nothing. I hit solid, but the creatures giggled and blew foul breath and grabbed at me, clawed my flesh, pulled my arms to their mouths like they were going to eat me.

The five of us fought with slashes of sword and stabs of spear and thrashing, wild frenzy, but we lost. Four of the creatures had me and were lifting me up, carrying me, up off my feet. I cried out but no one was there to help.

Another dream? Was this another dream? Happening to all of us. Was this real? Could it be real?

The creatures were carrying me, not eating me, just still poking and prodding and making the motions of eating, as though they were teasing. And all the while shrieking and yapping like satanic monkeys.

All at once the four of them leaped and I flew, carried, writhing and yelling in their claws, up to a long, low branch. They ran along the branch and carried me easily higher, higher up into the dark shadows of the tree.

I heard the voices of my friends. Cries. Shouts. Threats. All of us were being carried up into the tree, all helpless to resist.

One of the creatures leered at me and spat out a long, sticky rope that wrapped itself around my neck, around my chest, around my body, winding me up, trapping me with arms pressed against my sides. I could barely breathe, every exhalation let the cord tighten. More sticky cord, webbing, that's what it was, they had become spiders with eight arms and laughing, leering, slavering faces.

I was wrapped, on my back, tied immobile and gasping to a thick branch.

A dream? Where was the hole, where was the flaw, the internal inconsistency? The other dream had made less sense. Then the pain had not matched the facts; here it did. I felt everything. Everything as I should feel it. No flaw. No telltale inconsistency.

Real. It was real. This time Eshu had tired of warning dreams. This time he meant to kill us.

The spider creatures scampered over me, around, up and down the branches, celebrating their victory. I could see David, tied upside down to the trunk, bound as I was bound. I saw April's red hair hanging from a higher branch. Saw Senna's leg dangling free, kicking, then caught up with cords that moved with minds of their own.

They had us. One of the monsters stood on top of me, stuck his face down close to mine and vomited. The reeking mass covered my face, blocked my nose; I gasped for air but my mouth filled with the hideous goo. I tried to spit it out, but there was more and more.

I was woozy, mind slipping, consciousness fading, swirling, then air! I sucked it in, spit again, sucked air and filth inside me.

I was trying to get my hand into my pocket, trying to reach the Coo-Hatch knife that would cut anything, but I was held too tight. The cords had minds of their own. They sensed my efforts and tightened to stop me.

Then, a smell that brought with it a fear that reached deep down inside me and almost made me pass out. Smoke. Smoke. And now, heat.

They had set the tree on fire.

CHAPTER X

Flames licked up, red-tipped, yellow and gold, they rose beneath me. Twin agonies: fire and the fear of fire. I was going to burn. I was going to burn alive.

Flames raced up the tree's trunk, unnatural fire, too fast, too swiftly advancing. Up the trunk to stop just below David. Along the branches, as though someone had splashed the branches with gasoline.

I heard screams, inhuman and human. The demons danced in the flames, happy in their element. They filled their hands with fire and washed their faces with it and laughed at us screaming and crying and begging.

David's voice was a harsh bellow. Again and again. Or was that me? Some awful sound was coming from me, some sound I could never have willed, some sound that was squeezed from the darkest corners of my mind.

I choked on the smoke, on the demon's filth, on my own terror. *Let the smoke take me,* I begged, *let the smoke take me now, don't let me burn alive.*

Then . . . a swoosh, a blur of movement, a shimmering disk. It hit the tree trunk and kept on flying. The trunk slid down, bisected inches below David's feet. Sliced like a French-cut green bean, cut at an angle. More, more swoosh, swoosh, a blade passing through one of the creatures, leaving him unharmed but no longer laughing.

Swoosh, and I was falling. I hit the ground hard. The entire branch hit the ground, knocked the flames down in the temporary vacuum.

The Coo-Hatch!

The next blade came with shocking accuracy. It was a swooshing wind that cut the cords that bound me around the chest, cut with such precision that my skin, even my shirt, was never touched.

The cords slackened. I yanked myself free. Fire all around me, falling branches, the sky itself seemed to burn above me. The demons, or whatever they were, screamed and danced as if all this was both infuriating and wonderfully enjoyable. They cavorted in the flames and then formed into a circle that leaped and tumbled and rolled and giggled delightedly.

In the center of the circle, Eshu. An old man once again, but transformed. No longer dusty and stooped. He was tall and strong and laughing with obvious self-satisfaction.

I helped April untie herself and stand up. The two of us together helped Christopher. David had helped himself. He was advancing, sword drawn, toward the circle of evil spirits.

April yelled, "David, don't!"

"Like hell," Christopher said, and he located his spear and went with David.

David raised his sword high and brought it down in a devastating arc, straight down on one of the demons. Galahad's blade caught the creature where its neck met its shoulders.

The grinning, slavering head rolled across the grass, still laughing. It rolled and rolled till it hit the line of direct sunlight. The demon yelped a mocking cry, incinerated, and disappeared. His body danced on.

Christopher drew back his arm and launched his spear straight for Eshu. He was too close to miss. The spear's bronze point hit Eshu in the chest, just below his heart. Half the head sank in.

Eshu calmly plucked the spear out. No wound showed in his smooth, newly youthful flesh. He tossed the spear lightly into the air. It caught fire and burned to ashes before it landed at Christopher's feet.

"Why do you bring such troubles on yourselves?" Eshu asked.

The fire was gone. The smoke **was** swept away on a fresh breeze.

"Looks to me like you're the one bringing the trouble," I said.

Eshu shook his head regretfully. "You are blind and refuse to see. Who are you to ignore the gods? Who are you to refuse them their due?"

"What gods?" Christopher asked.

"The great high gods. And we humble Orisha."

David looked like a man torn between reason and violence. He wanted to take a swing at Eshu. But he'd seen what little effect a spear had on the not-so-old man.

"Just what is it you want?" David demanded.

The circle of demons dwindled and became nothing but spiders, albeit big ones, tarantula-size. They crawled into holes in the earth. I breathed a sigh. Looking up I saw spring-green leaves already growing on the stumpy burned tree. The cut branches, the sliced trunk were extruding roots, jerky worms and snakes that dug into the dirt.

Eshu smiled a placating smile. "A sacrifice is customary."

"What sacrifice? What are you talking about?"

Eshu seemed perplexed. Like we couldn't possibly be that dense. And some of us weren't.

April said, "He wants us to make a sacrifice. You know, like in the Bible: sacrifice a lamb or a goat or a pig or whatever."

"Probably not a pig," David said dryly. "At least not in the Old Testament." To Eshu he said, "That's it? That's what this is all about? We have to kill some sheep or whatever?"

"And offer it up in sincere sacrifice to the great high gods who made all this world. And their Orisha, who oversee the wild beasts and the hot sun and the evil spirits."

"Where are we going to get a sheep?" Christopher wondered.

"Show us something to sacrifice, old man, and we'll do it," David said, thoroughly disgusted.

"No."

I said it and heard an echo. April. We'd both spoken at the same moment. I was surprised. So was she.

I heard Senna sigh. She was just behind me. "Give him his sheep. Let's get past this."

"No," April snapped. "I don't make sacrifices to idols. Sorry, but that's not even a close call. 'Thou

shalt have no other gods before me.' No idols."
She hacked a smoke-inhalation cough. "No sacrifices to idols. I can't quote it verbatim, but that's
the basic idea. First and second commandments,
I think."

"You're joking," Senna sneered.

"No. You guys do what you want. I don't make
sacrifices to false gods."

"False? What's false about them?" Christopher
wondered. "They were kicking our asses pretty
well till the Coo-Hatch saved us." He looked
around. "Where are the Coo-Hatch, anyway? We
owe those boys. Now, come on, let's just give this
clown his dead sheep and move on. Me, I want to
be a long way from our happy dancing devil-
spiders before nightfall. Bad enough in daylight."

"I'm with April," I said.

"Say what?" Christopher complained. "Give
me a break, Jalil, you don't even believe in God. I
do and I'm willing to take my chances breaking a
commandment. I've broken most of the rest, why
not one more?" He laughed.

"I don't care about some commandment. That's
not what this is about. Eshu is trying to force me to
accept him and his particular gods as being the real
thing. I'm not going that way." I shook my head.
"I'm not going to bow down to his bunch of gods
or to Loki or to Huitzilopoctli or even to Athena.

Eshu here tried to scare me earlier; it didn't work. Won't work now. Sorry, but every time some immortal ass shakes a thunderbolt at me, I'm not going down on my knees."

Christopher threw up his hands. "Well, this is classic: We finally have April and Jalil on the same side. That side being the side of sheer, freaking stupidity. Joan of Arc and Jesse Ventura, together at last."

Senna spoke to Eshu directly. She sounded like a lawyer negotiating a contract dispute. "What will it take to keep your people happy? Three of us will gladly participate and offer whatever appropriate sacrifice is required. These two have a different view, but maybe we can reach some agreement anyway."

Eshu adopted a similar tone. "I am a lowly messenger. I bring the words of the high gods to man. And I remind man of his obligation to the Orisha." He spread his hands and smiled. "I demand nothing for myself, though I am one of the Orisha and most men . . . most sensible men . . . would offer sacrifice to me. But I can't surrender the claims of my brothers and sisters. And no one can speak for the great high gods."

Senna nodded. "Orisha are a sort of minor god?"

Eshu thought that over and nodded. "Yes. The

Orisha can be known and understood and named by mortal man. The great high gods are beyond understanding."

"Great, now I won't have to take that Intro to African Myths class when I get to college. Got it covered," Christopher said.

"You came together to this land," Eshu said. "You spoke against the gods of other lands. This angers us. Mortals must show respect for the gods. It is wise. It is prudent."

"Wait a minute," David said. "Now you're telling us what we can say?"

Christopher barked a laugh. "Here it comes. Here comes the First Amendment."

"A wise man does not speak contemptuously of the gods," Eshu said, eyes steely. "An unwise man may suffer many calamities in this dangerous world."

It was a clear threat and David's jaw clenched. "You don't tell me what to say. No one tells me what to say."

"First Amendment, meet Second Commandment and Chuckie Darwin here," Christopher said. Then, to Senna, "It's pitiful when you and I are on the same side, Senna. Makes me think I must be wrong."

"Three to two. No sacrifice," David said to Eshu. "You don't tell me what to say, and you don't tell April who to pray to, and you don't tell Jalil a damn thing."

Senna erupted. She was calmness itself most of the time, but Senna thwarted could be violent. "You idiots. You hopeless idiots. Where do you think you are? This isn't a church. This isn't America. And it's not Philosophy 101, Jalil. This is Everworld, you blind, stupid, ignorant, willful jackasses. You simpleminded, narrow morons, these aren't gods you argue about. You fight them if you have the power, and if you don't, then you do what they say." There was spit flying from her mouth as she ranted.

"Okay, four to one," Christopher said, shaking his head sadly. "It can't possibly be right to be on her side."

David had flinched as Senna exploded. But his eyes narrowed dangerously as she piled on the insults. It made me glad to see. Athena had forced Senna to relinquish her direct hold on David. He still loved her, the poor dumb fool, but he was no longer her tool.

"No, Senna, that's your view," David said when at last she paused for breath, red in the face and shaking. "It's all about power for you. Not me. Anywhere I go I have my rights. Go to Iraq, go to China, go to Everworld, I don't care, I have the right to say what I want, and April has rights and

so does Jalil. As a matter of fact, you know what?
I'm glad we cleared this up. Maybe we do have to
deal with these gods — doesn't mean we have to
buy their act."

I grinned at Eshu, deliberately provoking him,
making sure he realized he'd lost. But he seemed
perplexed, not defeated.

"Your words have no meaning," Eshu said.

"No sheep," I said. "No goat, no baboon, no
nothing. You're a messenger? Deliver this: We're
tired of being crapped on by every jerkwad with
magic powers. You want to try and kill us? Hey,
real experts have tried that and failed. You go tell
your high gods and your low gods and your middle gods and any other gods you have hanging
around that we're not their toys. We're men. And
women. And you know what else? We're Americans, and we fight for our rights."

It was a fine speech. We all felt pretty good as
Eshu walked off, shaking his head slowly. Defi-
ance is a wonderful thing. We headed off toward
Egypt, all aglow with our own righteousness.

All except Senna, who kept a prudent hundred
yard's distance between herself and us. As Christopher pointed out, she was keeping just outside of
thunderbolt range.

CHAPTER
XI

We walked, and the sun declined, and nothing happened except that we became more thirsty and more tired.

No, one thing happened: The sun slid down out of the sky, heading for a rendezvous with the horizon. Night was coming. The night of Everworld, a night without streetlights or headlights or the blue glow of TV screens. Hard-core night of the type that scared hundreds of generations of humans who could do little but huddle together and listen to the howling of wolves and the coughing roar of the leopard.

We tried to keep our righteousness high going, but it was a lost cause. Morality is a weak force. Fear is sharp steel and morality is a lace curtain.

"We better stop soon," David said. "Up ahead there."

"Where, in the jungle?" Christopher demanded.

We had reached the base of the densely green mountains. They remained as bizarre up close as they had been when seen from a distance. There was no fade from yellow grass plain to jungle slopes. It was as if someone had obsessively colored within the lines. Yellow here, green there. Period.

"No, not in the jungle, but near it," David said. "We'll need firewood and there isn't any out here. There should be some fallen branches just up the hill. Besides, look, you have totally different types of land, right? So maybe different animals. Maybe if lions come after us out here in the tall grass we can go into the jungle and they won't follow."

It was a sound-enough theory. I wasn't going to bet on it.

We found a tiny trickle of a stream coming down off the mountain and decided to flop there, just a hundred yards from the edge of the jungle. The line of trees exerted a heavy, depressing influence. Our recent experience in trees was not good. And these were ominous, dark, densely packed woods.

The mountain rose sharply, looming up to conceal whatever moon there might have been.

I volunteered to look for firewood. April joined me. The psychology was too obvious. We felt like whatever came down, it was our fault. We were in it together.

"Ever think maybe we should have just kept our mouths shut?" I asked as we stooped to gather bits of termite-riddled wood as near to the edge of the trees as we could stay.

"Oh yeah," she said. "Thinking it big time right now. What do you think will happen?"

"Something very bad," I said. "Eshu hit two of us with hallucinations. Then, when we didn't get it, he brought on those demons, those bad spirits, whatever they were. He's escalated already, and that was before we categorically blew him off."

"Whatever happens, we're the ones everyone will blame."

"And David," I said. "He was with us."

April smiled.

I stood up, heard my knees crack. "What?"

"I think maybe David was being a good leader. He saw the two of us were determined, so he took some of the burden on himself."

The idea had not occurred to me. "You think so? I'm not good at reading people."

"Most people have a problem accepting responsibility. David has a problem not accepting it. He's trying so hard to be a hero."

"You admire him."

"Don't you?"

"Yeah, I guess I do," I admitted. "He's scared. Even I can see that. Sometimes I watch him, waiting for his head to explode. Waiting for the meltdown. It's coming, sooner or later. Or maybe never, I don't know."

April nodded and went back to gathering wood. Her arms were full; she had to stoop to snatch up twigs with her fingers. The darkness that was sweeping across the grassland like a wave was already pooling beneath the trees.

"Let's hope if he melts down it's not tonight," she said.

"Yeah."

"What's up with the Coo-Hatch?"

I shrugged. "I think they protected their investment. They saw we were in trouble, and they want us alive. It's my one real cause for optimism. They're presumably still out there, and they still want to see us get to Egypt."

I heard a tromping sound and spun around, dropping my load of wood. My heart hit fast-forward and then I saw it was just Christopher.

"Napoleon sent me to cut stakes," Christopher said, jerking his thumb back toward camp. "I need to borrow Excalibur."

"Steaks?" April asked with a frown.

"Stakes. Little thin trees we can sharpen into points and stick in the ground and cower behind while we pee in our pants and pray to Jesus to rescue our sorry asses. Or in Jalil's case, cower, pee in pants, and recite some favorite quotes from Stephen Hawking, or whatever it is scared atheists do."

I laughed. The image was way too real. Way too likely. But we had another hour of half-light, which meant another half hour of bravado. "Stakes it is."

We hauled firewood and cut stakes and twisted them into the ground. They were of varying heights, as short as six inches above ground level, as long as two feet. Not as close together as we'd have liked, but there were two rows, and they were a fairly impressive palisade surrounding a camp no more than ten feet across.

We had a small fire going, with mismatched, rotting bits of firewood piled around like an inner wall. There was no room to walk. Barely room to lie down if we crunched together. I felt bad about the termites. Every time we'd throw a piece of wood on the fire they'd come pouring out only to be incinerated.

I guess where the termites were concerned, we were the careless, murderous gods.

We had David's sword, the remaining spears,

and my little knife. We had fire, and we had sharp sticks. And somewhere out in the swift-falling darkness, the Coo-Hatch with their inhumanly sharp and accurate throwing blades.

"I hereby christen this Camp Porcupine," Christopher said. "I'm for going to sleep and crossing back over to the real world and hoping for the best."

"Good idea," David said.

Christopher flopped on the ground and patted the ground on either side of him. "April, Senna? Room for both of you. I mean, if we're going to die, why not one final good-girl, bad-girl, sweet and bitter, saint and witch three-way? David and Jalil will promise not to look."

Senna ignored him entirely. She had joined our camp only with highly visible reluctance. She held us all in contempt, that much was obvious. And it kind of comforted me. I enjoyed the fact that she had to choose between being all alone in the night and being with us.

"No good choices, huh, Senna?" I said. "Out there with the wild animals, in here with the fools?"

She favored me with an acid glare. Then she laughed derisively. "Go to sleep, Jalil. It will be nice to cross over and get a chance to clean up."

I said nothing. Tried to show nothing. Senna

knew that in the real world I was obsessive-compulsive. It was her weapon to use on me. The threat to tell the others, to show me up as weak and pitiable was always there. It hung over me. I was determined not to let her bully me. But as much as I might pretend otherwise, I feared ever having the others find out.

I wanted to say something defiant. But I'd used up my quota of defiance on Eshu.

Senna smirked. She knew I was bluffing. She knew her threat worked, at least a little, which was all she needed in order to stick a sharp needle in me from time to time.

Senna turned away, sat with her narrow back to the rest of us, and looked out into the night. Or slept, I don't know. Maybe she didn't need sleep. Or wanted us to think she didn't.

David, as always, took the first watch. I would be next. I needed to fall asleep as soon as possible.

The fire was pitifully small. A tiny red-yellow eye winking in a vast and endless sea of darkness that filled the forest and the plains and covered every living thing.

April lay down beside me. I wondered if she was praying. It must be nice to have that comfort. Probably a bit more satisfying than just hoping, hoping that the Coo-Hatch could see in the dark and still cared whether we lived or died.

"Are you praying?" I whispered.

"Yes."

"For what?"

"Same thing I used to pray for when I was nine. A pony." She laughed, a sound that started low and rose to a silly giggle.

I took the laugh, drew it into me. That could be my own form of prayer, I thought: a scared girl laughing at the night.

There were times, not many, but times when I kind of liked the human race.

Chapter
XII

Once again, though, that glow of good-feeling didn't last long. The shelf life for optimism is about eight minutes in Everworld. David squatted beside me and gave me a look that made me sigh without knowing precisely why.

"Come on," he said. "I need you. You and I need to take a walk."

"Why?" I was tired. Not interested in playing games.

"We're going to visit the Coo-Hatch. I need you to watch my back."

I got up reluctantly, stumbled to catch up with David who was already striding purposefully into the dark as though there was nothing to fear.

When I caught up to him he confided our mission. "I want to check on our Coo-Hatch friends.

I want to thank them. Find out what they're up to. They invited us."

"Invited us? When did that happen?"

He stopped, pointed. "See that little glow right there? That's the glow of a fire. The Coo-Hatch. You think the Coo-Hatch don't know we can see that fire? They know. You think they couldn't hide it, if they wanted? They could hide it. They want us to see the fire."

"Why?" I asked.

"I don't know. But I can guess. First time we met them Christopher said they were businessmen. He was right."

I didn't press him. I've grown to trust David's instincts in certain areas. Only in certain areas.

We traipsed through a night so dark that I actually tried holding my hand up and testing whether I could see it. I could. Barely. What I couldn't see was the ground. I could be stepping on a scorpion, a snake . . . I could be stepping on a lion. I walked with the expectation of being tripped at any moment.

Suddenly, a whoosh of air right by my ear. A bird or a bat had flown past, very close. The words "vampire bat" were suddenly lit up in neon letters in my brain. I cringed, drew my hands up around my head and neck.

"It's one of them," David said. "One of the young ones."

It took me a moment to stop imagining tiny bat teeth in my neck and realize he was talking about a juvenile Coo-Hatch.

"It's been following us for a while," David said, unable to keep the smug sound out of his voice.

"What, do you see in the dark now?" I grumbled.

He laughed. Laughed like we were doing nothing more dangerous than sneaking home late to avoid waking our parents. "Carrots. Always eat plenty of carrots. Anyway, they know we're coming. That's good. We don't want to surprise them."

The fire was brighter now, easy to see. But still I had the sense we were seeing only reflections of light and not the light itself. That was, at least, till we stopped just in time at the edge of a shallow ravine. A dry river bed, I guess.

And down there, in that narrow space, a dozen Coo-Hatch adults, "Grouchos" as we sometimes called them. Eleven of them were hard at work around a large and intense charcoal fire that was contained within an oval ring of half-buried stones. The heat and light of that fire reminded me strangely of a tape I'd seen once, a night shot of magma rolling across a Hawaiian landscape.

Two of the Grouchos worked a large bellows, fanning the flame. The rest were laboring to rig a rope harness around a six foot long, ornate, tapered cylinder.

The cylinder was an antique. But a brand new antique, fresh from the forge, fresh from whatever process the Coo-Hatch used to temper their metal.

It was a cannon. Something you'd see on a visit to a Civil War battlefield. Or earlier, I suppose. A cannon you might have seen on a Spanish galleon.

The ropes, the block and tackle, were obviously to be used to lift the cannon into a two-wheeled carriage made of fresh-cut wood.

The one Coo-Hatch not hard at work Groucho-walked up to us from the side. He'd been waiting. He didn't seem very comical, outlined against the fire of the forge. The squashed "C" of his body, the elongated nose, the buggy blue in red eyes all seemed even stranger, even more unworldly than the first time we'd seen one of these creatures.

"You came," the Coo-Hatch said. "We are Coo-Hatch of the Fifth Forge. We are also Coo-Hatch of the Ninth Forge, come together by chance in this place. I am Tashin."

"You're not the one who was at Olympus."

"No. He is also of the Fifth Forge, but not with us."

"You saved our lives," David said. "We are grateful."

"We saved your lives," Tashin agreed. "You owe a debt."

"Uh oh," I muttered.

"How can I repay that debt?" David asked. None of this was surprising him. Nor was it bothering him. He was after something of his own.

"We have little experience in handling large objects," Tashin said.

"Yeah, I can see that. That cannon must weigh half a ton. And the tackle you've set up will snap in a heartbeat. You want me to help you mount the cannon on the carriage?"

"That would pay your debt," the Coo-Hatch said.

I almost laughed. It was amazing at one level. The Coo-Hatch could create a steel superior by far to anything that could be achieved in twenty-first century America — and do it while on the move through a forbidding landscape — but they couldn't tie decent knots? Technology doesn't move in a smooth, orderly fashion.

"You happen to run into some fellow Coo-Hatch so you just decide to make a cannon?" I asked.

I guess Tashin saw how that might seem weird. "We meet by chance, we pool our knowledge. Each Forge comes away the wiser."

"I can help you handle the cannon," David said. "Providing you ropes are good. I can show you the knots, I can help you put together a block and tackle."

"Then all debts would be paid," the Coo-Hatch said with what was probably Coo-Hatch courtesy.

David didn't move. "You intend to continue following us?"

"We are interested in your success," Tashin said diplomatically. "It has fallen to this cohort of the Fifth Forge to observe your progress."

"Fair enough. You know, we may profit from your help in the future. I would hate to ever find myself unable to repay you."

Tashin nodded, waited, a businessman knowing he was about to hear an offer.

David looked at me, as if asking my permission to proceed. But I was in the dark, clueless. What was he up to? Making sure the Coo-Hatch would help us if needed? They would do that anyway.

"The cannon there. Is the bore smooth?"

The Coo-Hatch tilted his long snout sideways, quizzical. "It is as smooth as we can make it. The ball that is fired will suffer very little resistence."

"Too bad," David said. "Because, see, the ball will fly further and fly straigher, if you rifle the barrel. You cut shallow grooves into the bore, twisting. A loose spiral. Maybe one full three-sixty, doesn't take much. It makes the ball or shell spin. The spinning keeps it flying straight and true."

Tashin hesitated, not sure if David was jerking him around, I guess. "We will test this idea. If it is true, we will be in your debt."

David nodded. "It's true. Come on. Let me show you how to make a half-hitch."

For two hours David worked with the aliens, shirt off to handle the heat from the forge. He's an amateur sailor, and I guess all sailors know their knots. I was almost useless aside from following orders, pulling when I was told to pull, heaving when I was told to heave.

It was still blackest night when we left the Coo-Hatch with their cannon securely mounted. We headed back, physically weary and dehydrated as well as sleepy.

"Okay, I'll ask. Why?" I said, once we were well away from the Coo-Hatch camp.

"What do you mean? We owed them."

"No, why tell them about rifling the barrel?"

He seemed unwilling to answer for a while. Then, "I'd rather you didn't talk about this to April or Christopher or Senna. Especially April. She'll just see us interfering more, bringing more weapons into Everworld."

"That's what you're doing," I said bluntly. "The question is why?"

He smiled, white teeth in the inky black. "Smooth bore cannon would never do it, Jalil. Remember Ka Anor's city? Junkie Dream mountain? I said if we had artillery we could sit there on the rim of that crater and bang hell of that termite mount? Well, smooth-bore won't fly that far, my friend. But you rifle it, you go to a cylindrical shell and you rifle it, and yeah, we can sit there on the rim and blow hell of the big bug house." He laughed a dangerous laugh.

"You know, I guess I should admire your foresight. But it just makes me think this is all going to go on too long. You wear me out, man. I'm beat and you're planning D-Day."

"We're almost back. You can sleep soon. You get some good z's you'll see the possibilities."

He was positively jolly.

CHAPTER
XIII

CNN: Breaking News.

Now what? I wondered. The near burning in the demon tree sent a shudder through me, an actual, physical shudder. I clutched my hands together on my desk to stop them from shaking.

I was in school, sitting in calculus class, watching the back of Miyuki's head and occasionally glancing at the blackboard. Class was almost over. The bell would ring any minute.

I had decided this was the place to ask Miyuki out. This was where she knew me, our one area of common ground. I'd been steeling myself for the ordeal. And then, just as I was tensing up and practicing my carefully casual lines and planning my graceful exit strategy for when she said no, it was time for the update from Everworld.

I was asleep, surrounded by sharp sticks, stalked

by some minor African deity with a grudge because we didn't want to kowtow to him and his fellow immortals.

Great. A crapstorm was going to come down on the other me. Once again, there was the pressing question of what happened to me if Everworld Jalil died. Once again, no way to know.

It all made me tired. Too tired to think about asking Miyuki out. This wasn't the time. Too much going on over there, over in my other life.

"Yeah, right, Jalil, just give up on this life. Why even bother. Just crawl into bed and wait for the updates."

Everworld was eating away at my real-world life. I lived here, in school, at home, at work, in the world of parents and friends and homework and counting the cash in your pocket to see what, if anything, you can do on a Saturday night. But into my brain flooded images of another life. Images that were so startling, so vivid, so electric that they made my own present-day life seem like the distant memory.

I was playing *Pong* in this universe and rocking with Lara Croft in the other.

The bell rang, I jerked in surprise, and the teacher began yelling out the assignment as all of us surged toward the door, already dismissing him from our onrushing lives.

"Just do it, Jalil. Just do it," I told myself. "Great, I'm a Nike commercial."

I sucked in a deep breath and slid past a pair of seniors to catch her. I fell into step beside her.

"Hi," I said.

"Hi."

"Um, my name is Jalil."

"I know that." She laughed, a little derisively. Not good.

"Good class, huh?" There you go, Jalil, that was smooth.

She nodded, glanced at me like I might be on the edge of becoming a problem in her life.

Screw it. Walk away. No. No, don't walk away.

"Miyuki? I was thinking maybe sometime, if you wanted to, we could study together. Or else go on a date."

What? That wasn't the way I'd practiced.

"Which one?" she asked.

I shrugged, a casual act that might possibly have fooled a blind man. "Which one? Either one would be fine with me."

She stopped walking, faced me, glanced over her shoulder. "I can study with you, but I can't go out with you."

"Oh. Okay."

"It's not personal. It's just, my parents are old country, you know? I mean, you know I'm not

Japanese-American, right? I'm Japanese. We're only here for a while. My dad works for a Japanese bank in the city. My real home is in Hiroshima."

Hiroshima. That was a name to make you wake up. "Wow. So that whole atom bomb thing, they don't want you dating Americans?"

She looked amused at that. "My parents weren't even alive then; do the math, Jalil. They don't care about that. They just don't want me dating American boys. They don't think American boys are serious enough."

That made my jaw drop. Then I laughed. "Miyuki, I'm probably the most serious person in this school. People make fun of me for being serious. Trust me, there isn't anyone more serious about school and so on than I am."

She looked up at me, a distance of close to a foot. She was not tall. I am.

"We could study together," she said. "At my house. Maybe my parents would change their opinions."

"Yeah? Okay, that would be cool." I smiled. "But if you could, you'd go out with me?"

"I don't know, Jalil. You're awfully serious for me." She laughed a teasing laugh and I was basically, as of that moment, in love.

I levitated through the crowd, untouched, unbothered by the common herd. Cool. She was willing to try and turn her parents around. More than cool.

Clearly she wanted me. Well. All right. Uh-hunh. Cool.

I opened my locker and began quickly arranging the books and notebooks in precise order, not even bothering to try and fight the compulsion. Books precisely centered, spines facing out, largest on the bottom, smallest on top. Three notebooks with the spiral wires stepped back so none touched the spiral below it.

I opened one of the little antibacterial wipes and wiped my fingers, one by one, careful not to miss any part. Little finger of the left hand through thumb, then a fresh wipe for the right hand.

I stuffed the used wipes back in their envelopes, careful that each went back into the envelope it had come from. Now to throw the wipes away without having to touch the trash can.

I closed the locker with my elbow, walked quickly to the boys' room, timed my approach perfectly so that the door was still open as I slid in behind some tenth grader.

I dropped the towelettes in the trash and checked myself in the mirror till I could escape the room without having to dirty my hands.

Obsessive-compulsive disorder. I was crazy, I thought, but yeah, I was serious. I was serious enough for a Japanese banker.

Miyuki. She seemed very clean. I wondered if she was like me. I knew there were others with OCD. Would it be a good thing or a bad thing if she shared my mental twist?

I headed for my next class, passed David on the way.

"Had an update lately?" he asked.

"Probably more recent than you," I said. "You're on guard. I'm catching Z's."

"Yeah? What am I looking at when the news breaks?"

"We were almost burned to death in a flaming tree by a bunch of demons."

He took a deep breath, absorbed the insanity, nodded very businesslike. "I take it we escaped?"

"Maybe," I said. "At the moment we're squatting in the dark waiting to see if we live till morning. But I got a date, kind of anyway."

"Well, as long as your social life isn't suffering," he said. "Man, I've got Jerden next. She loves to bust my balls and I'll be getting a flaming demons CNN in the middle of it. Crazy life, man."

"Her name is Miyuki. Her father doesn't like American boys because we're not serious."

He grinned, a rare thing. "Yeah, that's a problem for you, Jalil. You are the original wild party boy. Later, man."

I realized something that had never occurred to me before: David here was a different person from David there. It was subtle. Minor. Nothing that jumped out at you. But Everworld David and real-world David were diverging, growing apart.

And then, with a shock, I knew: So was I. Of course I was. We all were. It was inevitable. We, the two Jalils, were having different experiences. We transmitted memory, and that kept the changes from becoming radical, but the change was happening. Had to. We were living different lives, adapting to different environments. I tried to cling to all that I knew and believed here, but was it all really relevant to Everworld Jalil?

Would it have killed me to sacrifice a sheep?

"Pretty late to ask that, Jalil," I told myself.

And then, I woke in Everworld, and all hell had broken loose.

CHAPTER
XIV

The lightning was a bombing run. Like the old tapes of World War Two, with the waves of massed bombers overhead, dropping their sticks of bombs, rolling thunder, exploding in a fitful wave, louder, softer, all at once or one at a time.

Destruction moved toward us, lightning slashed down from a black sky, punctured the earth again and again, trees suddenly torches, visions of animals incinerated, cooked by a flash of unimaginable energies.

"That's a bitch of a storm," Christopher said. His blond hair was ruffled by the wind.

We all were standing, the five of us, all cramped together in our pitiful little fort, all watching the awesome display. A wave of fire, a chomping jaw of jagged electric teeth.

"That's no storm," Senna said.

"No," I agreed. "It's too narrow. Clear sky and stars to the left and right of it."

The sound was of bombs exploding. Explosion on explosion, ground shaking, reverberations that became part of the following explosion, one on another till there was only one vast, unending explosion.

"We'll lie down, we'll be okay," David said doubtfully. "Lightning takes the shortest path, right? It'll hit the sticks. We stay low . . ."

There was a crack like the sound the earth itself would make if it split in half.

"That assumes that lightning in Everworld follows the same rules," I pointed out.

Christopher cursed.

"Into the trees," April suggested.

"You're not supposed to stand under trees in a storm. They attract lightning," Christopher said.

Senna laughed. "No, *we* attract lightning. You don't get it. That's our lightning. All for us. As long as it can find us it'll kill us. We stand out here, that storm will come and sit right over us."

"If Eshu wanted to kill us, why have the storm creep up on us?" David said. "We could already be dead. I'm worried this is about moving us. That storm is supposed to get us to run."

He was yelling to be heard above the noise. The

wind was growing in strength, snatching our words from our lips.

"Cat and mouse," April said, using both hands to keep her hair out of her face. "Maybe they enjoy watching us run for our lives. Maybe that's the thrill."

David shook his head, unsure, undecided.

I said, "David, maybe Eshu figures he wins either way: We stay put, he fries us; we move, he goes to plan B."

"Yeah," he said, nodding at me and sending me a look of gratitude. "You're right. Plan A or Plan B. I'm not crazy about Plan A. Hard to do much against lightning. Let's head for the trees."

"And leave all our sharp sticks?" Christopher complained.

"Let's go."

We sidled through the barrier of sharpened sticks, careful not to impale ourselves on our own pitiful defenses. Lightning painted us electric blue and etched black shadows. Senna's face was lit and shadowed, a Halloween mask. A flash, and our sharp sticks seemed to jump, to jerk manically as the flashes came like strobes.

The line of trees was close. We didn't run, didn't want to run because running breeds panic.

But then it was as if the lightning spotted us. The storm whipped into a sprint, racing across the ground, light and sound all melding into one phenomenon, a racing, continuous explosion.

"It's after us!" Christopher yelled.

"Run!"

We ran. Ran for the trees and the storm flew after us. A hundred yards. Fifty. Ten and the storm blew our camp apart with a single jolt from the sky. The sharp sticks flamed, a double row of matches.

A dam in the sky was breached. A billion gallons of water poured down. Fat raindrops slapped and stung, hammered and bruised. Everything was mud, slippery, foot-grabbing, plastering mud.

Then, a tree I reached, an earsplitting explosion and the tree blew apart, blew apart into flaming splinters, and I fell, deafened. I hit the ground, scrambled up, ears ringing, blood gushing from my nose.

Up, a flash of April as another tree flamed. Vines grabbed at me, the hill itself fought me, gravity relentless, trees burning, erupting, the thunder that seemed to come from the ground itself, like being an ant walking across a bass drum.

"Over here!" David's voice, half drowned in the next explosion.

Over where? I couldn't see him. All I saw were floating traces of light, like having a flashbulb go off in your face a hundred times. Saw only shadows and sudden, brilliant, blinding blue stark outlines.

"This way! This way! There's a cave."

A cave. Yeah, yeah, that would do it. But where?

"This way!" David kept yelling.

And all at once I stumbled into him, his black hair in his face, eyes blinking, water rushing into his open mouth as he screamed right in my face. "Down there. Down there."

He gave me a shove, pushed me down on my knees, and I tumbled forward, slid in the mud, and I was rolling, sliding, which end was up?

I came to a stop. Slammed into Christopher. April was just behind me. But there, already down in the cave, in a flash of lightning from above, I saw David.

David was here. How was David here?

Who had grabbed me and pushed me down here?

"Eshu!"

Senna slid, cursing, to land in our wet, filthy pile of arms and legs, and right behind her, a gushing wave of mud that blocked out the light and the sound and washed up around our feet, our ankles, our legs, up to our waists.

The mud rose, rose to choke the life from us.

CHAPTER
XV

The mud was a living thing, a murderous force. It forced me down, pushed me, rolled over me, covered me, smothered me, lifted me, and swept me away.

It was in my nose, eyes, ears, mouth. It billowed beneath my clothing, squeezed into my shoes. I weighed a thousand pounds. I moved like a man asleep. I moved like a slow-motion special effect, swimming in pudding.

I held my breath, lungs burning, tried to spit the stuff out of my mouth only to have the pressure of the mud fill my mouth further and threaten to force its way down my throat to clog my lungs and bloat my stomach.

All at once I was atop the wave, floating, uplifted on a rushing river of mud. I was a bit of bark tossed along on the rushing stream, not sinking but threatening to be swallowed up by ripples and currents and eddies.

Down a tunnel. Through the bowels of the earth, racing beneath a low rock ceiling, and then, all at once, sunlight!

The ground vomited me up and I was turned around, lost, dazed, upended. I had the illusion that the mud flow was suddenly above me, that it was flying over my head, even though I was still in it, still stuck in the goo.

I felt I had to grab onto the mud, had to clutch at it to keep from flying straight down into the sky.

Then the mud washed me up, like a murderous tsunami that in the end comes to little more than a rush of foam on the sand. I was a beaten, barely survived surfer, staggering up/down, falling, no, falling upward, what was happening?

The sky, bright Clorox white and flecked with blue clouds, was below me, under my head. I was standing but my feet couldn't possibly stick to the ground, couldn't, could not, because I knew that it was all upside down.

I felt the sky beneath me. I saw the sun, black and yet bright, shining in a white sky, peeking around baby-blue clouds.

"What the holy crap is going on?" Christopher yelled.

I saw him, like me, seemingly glued to a ground that had become a ceiling. I cringed, knelt, tried to fight the absurd urge to grab onto the ground, to clutch big handfuls of the royal-blue grass.

I fought it. Impossible. The ground had to be below me, the sky had to be above. *Don't be stupid, Jalil, you're not falling toward the sky. Gravity is still toward the ground, that hasn't changed.*

But everything had changed. I was in danger of falling straight down into a sky as white as a blank page. I could fall into the black sun.

I saw the others. Each covered in filth, each dragging themselves up or crawling or cringing, all looking fearfully at the sky below, all holding, or wanting to hold onto the ground itself lest they fly off.

I closed my eyes. That was the way. That was it, the only way to fight the illusion. Blinded, I could keep from throwing up. Blinded I could believe everything was where it should be.

"Close your eyes," I croaked, spitting mud. "It helps. Close your eyes."

"Okay, my eyes are closed," Christopher said. "Now someone tell me what the hell is going on here. What is this, Alice in Wonder-freaking-land? Where's the big white rabbit? Where's the caterpillar with the hookah? 'Cause absolutely nothing is going to make this any weirder."

David, his voice shaky but trying to project whatever stability and sanity he could manage, asked me, "Jalil, man, you get this?"

"No, I don't," I said shortly. "I feel like I'm upside down. Or else like everything else is. I know gravity is holding me to the ground but I can't lose the feeling that the ground is up and the sky is down."

I pried open my drying-mud-caked eyes and peeked again. The illusion came back full force. I heard someone puking, but that was the last thing I needed to see: vomit falling down into the sky. Actually, it would fall to the ground.

"It's a sight thing," I said. "I mean, I feel that down is down. My arms aren't trying to relax toward the sky." I tried a small jump, feeling idiotic. A small jump, just to see whether I fell into the sky. I landed on the ground.

"It's a visual thing," I repeated more confidently, but with my eyes closed for sanity's sake.

"It's a reverse image," April said. She sounded close. "It's not just the upside-down thing. The sky is the color of clouds and the clouds are the color of sky. The sun is black, not white or yellow. The grass is blue. It's all the reverse, all the opposite."

"White sky is not the reverse of blue sky," I said, sounding pedantic even to myself. "Black sun is not the opposite of a yellow sun. Blue grass is not —"

"Stop being literal," April interrupted excitedly. "It's not science, it's . . . it's poetry. Poetic opposites. I mean, whoever came up with this didn't know about the light spectrum. They just thought, *What would be the opposite of whatever?"*

"Yeah," David agreed dubiously. "It's opposite world or whatever."

True enough, I thought. Yes, not a scientist's idea of opposites. A simpler mind. Less concerned with abstract notions of truth and accuracy. Not a modern vision, an older one.

"It's the gods," I said disgustedly. "It's right about their level of thinking: Primitive. Irrational. Inconsistent."

I was surprised to hear Senna laugh. "You just don't ever learn, do you, Jalil? You really think this is a good time to be insulting the gods?"

"I gotta go with the witch on this," Christopher muttered. "I'm thinking next time someone says, 'Kill a sheep for the gods,' just kill the sheep. Crazy mothers want a dead sheep, let's give them a dead sheep."

"It's a mirror world," Senna mused. "A subtle

notion of an afterlife, don't you think? The details are inconsistent, but it was a fascinating idea."

"Hey, let's stand around on our heads and admire it all," Christopher said shrilly. "Senna and Jalil and April, you three can lead the discussion. Me, I'm going to grab onto this dirt so I don't fall off the earth and go flying off into space."

"What do we do?" April asked.

"I don't know," David admitted. "This is . . . new. Can't get back to where we want to be, the tunnel or hole or whatever is all plugged up with mud. No way back through there."

Senna said, "Well, well, finally a situation where Mighty Davideus admits he's lost."

"You have a plan, Senna?!" Christopher snapped, coming to David's defense.

"Yes, actually. Let's find a stream and get washed off."

"How are we supposed to walk anywhere?" April demanded.

Senna laughed, a surprisingly happy sound. "It's hard for you, isn't it? The four of you, so normal and conventional underneath it all." She spread her arms wide. "It's magic, boys and girl. Magic! Welcome to my world."

She didn't quite twirl around in girlish delight, but she looked like she wanted to.

"We do have to get this mud off us before we end up baked solid," I said. "There must be water, or something like it."

"Yeah, let's all find a nice bath," Christopher agreed. "And by the way, if anyone sees a sheep, fold your Ten Commandments and your Constitution and stick them right up your butt, then kill the damn sheep."

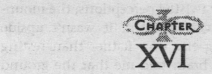

CHAPTER
XVI

We found a stream, but we weren't happy at what we found.

Our view of the broader landscape had been blocked by a stand of trees, weirdly identical to normal trees, aside from being orange. But once we stepped out from behind the screen of trees we saw the mountains. Much the same as the mountains we'd seen on the other side of this mirror-image world, with one crucial difference.

"Oh, man," Christopher moaned.

We stopped, stared, fought down the renewed urge to blow lunch into the sky. The vertigo was so distorting that at first I could make no sense of what I was seeing.

The mountains were upside down. They were rough triangles, like any mountain, but with the point resting on the ground, and the vast base ending in midair.

The entire mass looked as if it had to tip over, had to fall, had to crush everything beneath it with the unimaginable impact of a billion tons of earth.

And yet, to my twisted perceptions, the mountain seemed perversely right. It wasn't upside down, everything else was. Rather than resting on its point, my brain told me that the ground was the sky and it was resting instead atop the mountain.

A stream flowed from the mountain. It flowed uphill, actually down the mountain, moving from the base of the mountain to the peak, at which point it flowed seamlessly out onto the flat ceiling/floor of blue grass.

"I guess there's no need to point out that this totally screws with the laws of gravity," I said.

"No, I think we all sort of noticed that," David said.

"It doesn't cast a shadow," April pointed out.

She was right. The mountain, with a mass of five hundred great pyramids all balanced like a kid's spinning top, should have blocked out the sun. But it did not.

"I'll say one thing for these African gods: The boys do strange really well," Christopher said.

"Their minds are free," Senna said admiringly. She was as close to happy as I've ever seen her. "They aren't hemmed in by the limits of conventional thought. They're like . . . I don't know. So simple they're sophisticated. So basic they're brilliant. Look at this world! What is Hel's domain compared to this? Hel's a crude killer. This, now this is art."

"Art?" David echoed.

"Art. Not science, art. Not technology. This is magic practiced by gods who were left alone by their mythologists. Pure creation, pure, simple ideas realized. I can learn from this."

Christopher said, "Oh, good, it's Disney World for witches. I'm *so* glad Senna is happy. There's a mountain the size of Michigan upside down, right side up, tippy-topping over our heads, and a lovely stream of nasty purple water, and all is right with the world. Let's all go skinny-dipping and lie out upside down in the bright black sunlight."

One way or the other, we had to wash off the mud. It wasn't optional. I could barely move. It was in my pants. It wasn't an obsessive-compulsive thing, this was a necessity.

April went a few dozen yards one way, walking like we all did, like creeping along bent over would keep us glued to the ground. Senna went the other direction. Which left the three guys in the middle, a bit embarrassed about how not to accidentally spy on one or the other of the two girls.

Truth was, we had other things on our minds. Even Christopher. There was the impossible-to-ignore sense that the stream, although it was down by our feet, was actually up over our heads. I had to fight my mind's urge to believe that the water might begin to spill down over me like a shower. At the same time I was able to see the actual origins of the spring almost directly overhead as it flowed up/down the mountain before executing its impossible right angle to flow out toward us. Part of the stream was in reality above us, defying the laws of gravity, and the broader run of the stream was at our feet, appearing to our twisted perceptions as if it were defying the laws of gravity.

"Lucy in the Sky with Diamonds," David muttered.

I stripped off my muddy clothes and had to decide who to turn away from, Senna or April. I turned my back to April. I could never let it look like I needed to hide from Senna. At the same time I tried to blank out my field of vision beyond the immediate needs of sloshing my clothes in the water.

Christopher supplied the obvious solution: He waded into the purple stream, waist high, then squatted down and worked his clothes in the current. I followed him in. David stayed on the bank and kept a watchful eye for danger.

"David's peeking," Christopher said in a stage whisper.

"No, I'm not," David said angrily.

Christopher laughed and swooshed his clothes.

I ducked under the water to try and clean my hair. I scrubbed at my face and dug a finger in my ear. So strange that it was enough. So strange that the compulsions did not come. I could wash once. Not seven times. Not again and again, fighting the need, fighting for control over my own mind.

I stood up, shook my head, throwing off clean water now. Or as clean as purple water could be. And in that moment, not expecting it, I saw Senna in profile. I looked away immediately, but the image was there in my mind. Deliberate? Had she wanted me to see her as a vulnerable, lovely girl? Had she wanted me to respond with automatic desire?

Surely. Of course. Nothing was accidental with Senna. Was it? Disturbing. I could try not to respond, but I was not able to be indifferent. I could not pretend that my rational mind was all that was involved.

I tried to turn my thoughts to Miyuki. No. That was going the wrong way. I just ended up imagining Miyuki standing in profile, outlined against an impossible backdrop of breeze-bent blue grass.

I dressed in sopping wet, semiclean clothes. Not easy. Not exactly pleasant, but better. The grit would be with us for a long time.

David finally entered the stream, leaving his sword behind, leaned against a tree. I stared doggedly up at the absurd mountain that hung above us.

"Hey," I said, and pointed. "Look."

There were three canoes or dugouts or whatever they were called racing along the stream far overhead. Upside down, although I felt more like I'd fall up into them than the reverse.

"What?" David demanded.

"Up there. Canoes. Down there now, closer to the top of the mountain. The bottom. The pointy part."

David followed my finger. The canoes were moving swiftly, carried by the current and sped along by rowers stabbing the water with their oars.

"More good news," David complained and started to climb out of the water.

A scream. April! Not pain but surprise, fear.

I looked. She was clothed. Clothed and surrounded by two dozen tall black men, warriors armed with short spears and tall hide shields decorated with splashes of white paint.

David ran for his sword. Christopher snatched up one of the spears. A warrior stepped from behind the tree, swept his spear like a broom and knocked Christopher's legs out from under him. I ran toward Christopher, yanked the spear, and stood over him, face-to-face with the warrior. The warrior watched, poised, ready, but awaiting some signal.

David reached his sword at the same instant that three warriors leveled their spears at his chest. Maybe he would have fought some other time. But very few people are brave without their clothes.

April and Senna, both dressed now, were rounded up toward us. We were surrounded, bunched together, prodded by spears but not harmed.

The boss was easy to spot: He was not the tallest or the strongest. But he wore a leopard's skin draped over one shoulder and gathered at the waist. He had a phlegmatic look, unruffled, competent. He was at work and he knew his job.

He looked us up and down, paid particular attention to April's hair and to her backpack. He admired David's sword.

I don't know what I expected to happen next.
But what happened surprised me pretty well.

The warrior chief said, "Vikings."

"Say what?" Christopher blurted.

The chief ignored him and let go with a small
sigh. "It's a pity they can't be used. They are all
strong and would make good slaves. Unfortu-
nately, Vikings are animals. Kill him and him and
her; we'll keep the other two for the slower
death."

David, Senna, and I had been marked for death.

April and Christopher had been chosen for tor-
ture.

CHAPTER
XVII

In a very calm, reasonable voice, David said, "Do you mind if I get dressed first?"

The chief seemed surprised. But no, he didn't mind. David began to put on his clothes.

"We are not Vikings," I said.

"I have seen Vikings," the chief said. "I have fought many Vikings, and I have taken them as prisoners. They are new to our land, but I know a Viking when I see one."

"We are not Vikings," I repeated.

"You are perhaps not a Viking," the chief conceded. "But you travel with Vikings, so you are a Viking, too."

"There are many kinds of white men; not all are Vikings," I argued, wishing David would dress a bit more slowly. "These are not Vikings. These are called Americans. They come from another world."

This news did not seem to phase him. "Many come here from another world, and those who are here go into that other world. For all things are twinned, all things have two parts, a left and a right, a top and a bottom, a dark and a light."

David was almost dressed. He seemed calm. Usually David in a crisis gave off a palpable sense of danger, of being ready to erupt. But he was weirdly calm. So was Senna. Had the two of them seen something I'd missed?

I intercepted a glance between David and Senna. An almost imperceptible "get ready."

The boats, the canoes! Of course. I avoided looking upstream. Had the chief missed the approach of the canoes? Or were they his allies, his own men perhaps?

I shot a look at Senna, at the precise moment when she became the lion.

She let loose a roar that rattled the leaves in the trees. The warriors jerked in surprise. David leaped, grabbed his sword, hit the ground, and rolled to his feet. A spear stabbed, missed. David swung, horizontal, sliced the spear in half.

And then from out of nowhere came a roar that nearly equaled the roar of the illusory lion.

"For Mighty Thor!"

A huge man, a linebacker of a man with a battered tin-pot helmet, leggings, leather shirt, and goatskin vest, swung a notched ax up over his head and charged the chief.

The Viking bellowed, red-faced. Behind him came a motley collection of men, some white, some African, some Asian. Perhaps ten in all, no more than a third of the number the chief had. But the chief had been taken by surprise, first by Senna's magical lion, then by the suddenness of the onslaught.

The Viking berserker swung his big ax and a head hit the ground with a sick thump.

David swept in beside him and the battle was on. I grabbed a spear, one of our own long ones, and stabbed at the nearest foe I could reach.

The chief was taken by surprise, but he was a veteran. He rallied his retreating men, formed them in close, and came back at the Viking.

It was sheer, uncontrolled violence. Stabbing, slashing, yelling, axes and swords and spears and clubs all doing their brutal work.

I stabbed a man in the belly. I had to yank three times to free the blade, and with each yank the man cried out. We fought, the Viking and his strange crew all fought, the weight of numbers was telling against us. We backed toward the river. Backed up with nowhere to run. It would end very soon. I stabbed, I parried, I choked on my own fear.

No salvation, just a respite. No life saved, just a few extra seconds.

And then . . . Senna.

She had not fought, and the Africans had not bothered her, not even after she returned to her normal form.

Now she stepped forward and lifted up her hands. Her eyes were closed. She seemed indifferent, almost unaware of the carnage around her. She stood there, bathed it seemed to me in a light that touched only her.

The air around her was swirling, a slow-motion tornado, rippling, distorting the picture of her, twisting her into a wraith, a ghost, a memory of the lovely naked girl somehow melded to awful memories of Hel's horrible rotting flesh.

Both sides watched, fell back, stopped fighting, amazed, wary. Viking and African eyed one another, ready to resume battle if the other pushed it, but more fixated on this new phenomenon.

In a flash, the river churned up out of its course. The water dug a trench, ripped through the dry ground, a high-pressure hose blowing through mere dust. The water swallowed up the grass, churned the clods of dirt, ate bushes and saplings, and hit the Africans in a muddy tidal wave.

The entire river had changed course. One second behind us, the next racing right before me. The river channel behind us was nothing now but smooth wet rocks in a ditch.

The sudden onslaught caught most of the Africans flat-footed. The chief jumped clear, perhaps half of his men as well. But the other half, men who had been standing on bloody soil, now floundered in water that rushed over and around them, rose to their knees, waists, necks, and carried them screaming away.

The diverted river rejoined its old course. Of the fifteen or twenty men carried away there were now fewer than half a dozen still struggling to keep their heads above the mad torrent.

Senna lowered her arms, opened her eyes, and for a moment smiled as cruel a smile as it is possible to form with human lips. Her eyes were wide, bright, excited.

A purple river brown with churned mud now ran between us and the Africans. The chief stood, frozen for a long moment, then lifted his short spear and threw it with all his might. Straight for Senna.

David's sword flashed, caught the shaft, but instead of knocking it up and away he did what anyone would who thought the world was upside down: He slapped the spear down. The point grazed Senna's leg, cut flesh, drew a line of bright red across white calf.

Blood poured down into her shoes. She took three steps, then all at once she collapsed and fell to the ground in a faint. She lay in an undignified heap, sprawled ridiculously, helpless.

The African chief snatched a spear from one of his men, but he never got a chance to throw it. A long Greek spear appeared, the point deep in his belly.

I had thrown it without thinking, without knowing I had picked it up. An automatic response.

The chief looked surprised. Puzzled, as if he couldn't figure out why a bronze spear should be growing out of his chest. He staggered and fell, his body shaking uncontrollably. That was enough for his men. They broke and ran, all but two who stayed long enough to drag the chief away, groaning, clutching a wound that would kill him too slowly, too painfully.

A huge hand slapped me on the back and nearly knocked me down.

"Baldur himself never made a finer throw! By all the gods of Asgard, that was a fine throw for a minstrel!"

It took a moment for my brain to click. The dying chief was crying out in pain and anger as his frightened men dragged him roughly away.

I looked at the Viking. Then looked again.

"Thorolf?"

XVIII

The big man threw his arms around me and squeezed me tight before releasing me. "It is I, Thorolf!"

"No way. Dude!" Christopher said, grinning and pumping the old man's hand. "What the hell are you doing here?"

"You may well ask that," Thorolf said in a sharply subdued tone. "In this mad, upside-down place, nothing as it should. This is no place for a Norseman. By Odin's beard, they have no snow! And their ale is a poor substitute for the rich, foamy brew we love, eh?"

"I do love the rich, foamy brew," Christopher allowed, grinning happily.

David was kneeling beside Senna. She was moaning softly, stirring, beginning to revive.

David said, "Thorolf, you saved our butts there."

The Viking waved an embarrassed hand. "To be honest, I did not know it was you. I merely came to find another death in battle, but once again I have survived." He sounded weary, a little disgusted.

The part about "another death" took some digesting.

April said, "Thorolf, what do you mean 'another death'? And why are you trying to die in battle?"

"Break out the pitiful, womanly ale for my friends, you dogs," Thorolf bellowed goodnaturedly to his motley men. "These are the minstrels who escaped from Loki and saved us all from the filthy man-eaters. They will sing 'The Trampling Song,' then you will all hear." To us in a quieter voice he said, "I have tried to recall the words, to inspire my men, but only poor Lans remembered them all, and he died." Thorolf made a stabbing gesture toward his groin and made a pained face. Lans had died a hard death.

A man with one arm and one eye dragged a small wooden keg over to us. Thorolf twisted open the spigot, held it up over his head, and took a long drink. He offered it to David, who declined, at which Thorolf erupted into loud laughter.

"Of course, of course, you drink only the water, ah-ha-ha-ha, how we laughed at that jest."

His laughter was infectious. Despite all I'd just been through I found myself grinning. We'd been scared to death on first encountering the Vikings what felt like years ago. And the truth was, if they were your enemy you were in a world of trouble. But if they took a liking to you they could be generous, friendly, and almost childishly exuberant.

Thorolf had been the first Viking we'd met. We had stayed at his home, met his wife. We had gone off to fight the Aztecs together.

And for the song that Christopher had somehow managed to invent on the spot, Thorolf was our biggest fan.

David stuck to his abstemious ways, but I took a drink of the ale, and so did April. Thorolf was right: It was bad beer.

Senna woke fully, but sent very clear signals that she was not interested in talk. She sat alone, off by herself, thinking, pondering.

I wanted to ask her what had happened. Why had she fainted? The wound was superficial, and David had bound it up with some gauze we had swiped back at Olympus. I wanted to ask her whether it surprised her that she had the power to change the course of a river. It had surprised me. It had scared me. Still did.

Something drew my eye. An anomaly. Three

patches of dead grass. The three in a row. Each patch of the exact same size, roughly eight inches long and three wide. Footsteps. Senna's footsteps. Then another patch, more irregular, but with the grass just as dead, like it had been burned.

These facts registered, but my attention was yanked away by a loud guffaw from Thorolf.

Thorolf was telling his tale, under the influence of more ale. And his polyglot, Viking, Chinese, African, and who-knew-what-else crew were gathered around staring at us, leering at April, shooting worried glances at Senna, eyeing David's sword with professional interest.

They could all be Vikings, I reminded myself. The blond or redheaded Norse stock predominated among Vikings, but they had become a diverse bunch in Everworld, the result of traveling far and wide. Olaf Ironfoot, a great Viking leader, had been black.

"Well, after we made a slaughter of the sun-worshippers' city, killing all the Aztecs we could find, and oh, what a glorious day that was. I was ready to die that day, die the shameful death of a prisoner led to the slaughter, my heart to be fed to that foul, filthy thing, Huitzilopoctli." He shook his head, then brightened. "But you" — he swept his thick, hairy arm around to encompass us all —

"you saved the day and rescued Thor's hammer in the bargain. My good friend Christopher standing there atop the temple steps crying, 'Thor's hammer! Come on, you babies, let's kick some Aztec butt!' Ah-ha-ha-ha!"

"We were lucky," David said mildly.

"So, after the delightful slaughter, we who survived of the great army of poor old Olaf Ironfoot — who drinks now in Valhalla, bless him — we went into the jungle. I searched for you minstrels, but did not find you. Well, with our ships burned, off we went, looking for a way home."

He shook his head and his dirty matted beard. "It is truly worthy of a saga. We started out no more than two hundred men, and some women. We made war as we went, taking what we needed from the tribes, some of them no more fierce than lambs, but others as wild and dangerous as maddened boars! Ah, the battles we had there in the deep jungles."

He sighed at the happy memory. Vikings are a very pre-Vietnam culture. There's no ambivalence among them when it comes to war. War is what they do. War is what they love, win or lose, live or die. War and, of course, drinking, laughing, and boasting.

"So you had fun," I said.

"I am sorry you missed it," Thorolf said. "There were no more than fifty of us still alive by the time we left the jungle — all the rest had been gathered up by the Valkyries, borne off to deserved glory in Valhalla. And now we wandered, thirsty, lost, in empty lands. Some died a death no man should suffer. Finally, we were a handful, a mere twenty-one men, when we arrived in the land of the lions and the great gray monsters."

He made a hand motion that I took to be indicative of an elephant's trunk.

"And now, at last, we found meat, and foes worthy of our steel. We fought, always seeking a way home. We fought and always death avoided me." He shook his head regretfully at that. "Then, at a narrow gorge we were surrounded. Hundreds of them, the great, tall black ones. Oh, such fighters! They were all around us, in the hills, shutting off all hope of escape. We few sharpened our swords and prepared to die the death of men."

He zoned out, lost in memory. His eyes dreamed away; his mouth muttered silently.

"But you escaped again?" David asked.

"No," Thorolf said. "This big warrior, as big and black as that great king, Olaf Ironfoot himself, taller, though not as broad, pierced me through the heart with a spear even as I swept his head from his shoulders. Ah, but it was the death I've dreamed of since I was a sniveling child playing with a wooden sword."

"What do you mean? You died?" April asked. "I mean . . ."

Thorolf nodded, acknowledging the strangeness of his story. "It was a mortal wound. The spear sank as deep as Jalil's spear in that chief, but the aim was more true. It went in right here." He pointed at his heart. "I felt the clammy grip of death itself. And as I fell I beheld the Valkyries . . ."

His men were nodding, rapt. I realized I was holding my breath. And Senna was standing now, close enough to overhear, eavesdropping.

"I saw them, yes, and they were fierce and beautiful and rode their magnificent horses like men. Their hair was in long yellow braids. Golden armor covered their breasts, great golden helmets with eagle's wings adorned their heads. They shone with the light of the sun. The Valkyries came thundering, a sight that only the glorious dead may see. I held out my arm, ready to be seized and carried away to Valhalla. . . . But then the ground opened up beneath me. I and several of my fellow dead were carried down into the bowels of the earth and I heard an old man's voice speaking the words I can never forget: 'This is our land under the law of the gods. No sacrifice has been made, so sacrifice will be taken.'"

Thorolf looked thoroughly disgusted. "The Valkyries could not reach me. And when I opened my eyes again I was not dead at all, merely upside down in this strange land." He sighed and took another drink. "Since then I have done all I could to die a second honorable death, hoping that in doing so I would appease the gods of the old man. Surely then the Valkyries would come for me and bear me to Valhalla. But I live still. As do we all, Viking and honorary Vikings alike."

His men nodded glumly. They'd heard the story and, I guessed, lived various versions of it themselves.

"We'd like to get out of here ourselves," David said. "Although we came here without being killed in battle or otherwise."

"Yeah, we're here because certain people have inserted their heads in their butts and refuse to pull them out," Christopher said. "Tell you, though, from what I've heard about Valhalla I'm all for heading there next. Vikings know how to party. Not as well as old Dionysus, maybe, but Valhalla sounds like a cool frat at a major party school."

David rubbed his face, glanced at Senna, sighed. "Well, Thorolf, we're heading for Egypt. Long story there, too. But I wouldn't mind us all hooking up together. Maybe you can help keep us alive. And we can —"

"And we can try and get you killed," Christopher said.

"I was going to say that maybe we could find a way to get you to where you want to go," David said.

Senna said, "Eshu."

Thorolf looked at her in surprise. "This is Loki's witch?"

"That's her," April muttered.

"She has great powers," one of Thorolf's men said. "But she is not a hideous old crone."

"Yeah, well, beauty is only skin-deep," Christopher cracked. The men nodded thoughtfully, as if Christopher had said something not only profound but original.

"We met a local god of some sort, a minor deity," I explained. "He called himself Eshu. He appeared as an old man and said he was a messenger from the great high gods. Evidently he wanted us to make sacrifices to him and his gods. We refused. And here we are."

"Why would you refuse the sacrifice?" Thorolf wondered. "Could you not afford a goat or a lamb? Most gods will understand if you are unable to afford the animal. They will usually let you trade for a lesser animal, as long as you promise to make a larger offering later."

He might have been discussing the rules for paying credit card bills. Christopher gave me a look that said, *So, explain it to the man.*

I took that as a challenge. "Thorolf, we have certain beliefs that keep us from making sacrifices. At least April and I do."

Thorolf nodded as if he understood, but said, "It is right to honor the gods of each new land. Especially if they threaten you. No mortal ever wins a fight with a god."

April and I drew closer, unconsciously united in what seemed to everyone else to be our joint, if different, madness. But the truth was that I was starting to weaken. It was one thing to stand for a principle. It was another to drag other people down with you.

I said, "I think we have to find a way to get back to the normal world. I mean, the regular, right-side-up Everworld world. Thorolf died there. He is dead there. If we can get him back there then maybe the Valkyries will come for him. And we can go on our way."

"How exactly do we do that?" David asked.

"Well . . . well, this isn't some metaphorical, pie-in-the-sky afterlife; we're in a real place, and we got here by physical means. Down that hole. I think this is some kind of mirror-image world directly opposite the normal Everworld. I mean, I think the regular world is right under our feet. If we could dig."

"We fell like a hundred feet or whatever," April pointed out. "How are we supposed to dig that far?"

"I don't know," I admitted.

One of the Vikings, or quasi-Vikings, the black guy, spoke up. "There is a great tree that grows in both worlds. The roots join in the barrier between this world and the other. The tree grows tall here and there, seemingly two trees, but really one tree with two faces. Each tree has a trunk so thick that twenty elephants could not form a ring all the way around it."

"Digging through tree roots wouldn't be any easier than digging through the dirt," David said.

"You won't dig your way out," Senna said disgustedly. "Barriers of this sort cannot be crossed without supernatural intervention. And no, don't look at me, I don't know how to do something like that. Not yet, anyway."

An idea had begun to form in my mind. A small, mean idea. An idea that would leave Eshu no choice.

"They need this tree?" I asked the man who

had spoken. "I mean, these local gods, this is how they hold the two worlds together?"

"Yes, the tree roots unite and this bond holds all together."

"Yeah. Okay." I nodded, hesitant to broach my idea.

"Uh-huh, Jalil, are you getting ready to say something or are you just going to sit there looking like you might give birth at any moment?"

I shrugged. "Blackmail. They need the tree. The tree is vital. So we threaten the tree."

"Threaten to do what, carve our initials in it? You heard him say how big it is," David said.

"I don't know," I admitted. "Just seems to me that if the tree connects the two halves of this African world here, we should go to the tree."

"Yep, in principle," David said, nodding agreement. "Thorolf, do you know where the tree is?"

Thorolf didn't. But Senna did.

"I can feel it. I can sense the roots under our feet, and I can sense their direction." She paused, closed her eyes, and when she opened them again, she pointed away from the looming, upside-down mountain. "That way."

"And a little witch shall lead them," Christopher muttered.

We marched. Across the upside-down, reverse-world savanna. Through herds of slow-moving gazelles and racing elephants and zebras that wore yellow-and-pink stripes.

We walked beneath orange-colored trees filled with monkeys that made sounds like birds, and birds that chattered like monkeys. And we passed glowering lion prides, not visibly different from the lions of the regular world, whose rapacious females considered whether we would make a good meal for their cubs.

There were fifteen of us all told, a postapocalyptic street gang wandering between the African savanna and the African mountains, all of which were, in our heads, upside down. Not to mention the wrong colors.

We were as bizarre a collection of humans as has ever been assembled. The Viking and associate-Viking contingent looked like fugitives from a *Mad Max* movie. These were men for whom the end of the first millennium had never come, let alone the beginning of the third. They knew nothing of germs, genes, chips, waves, photons, quanta, light-years, millions, or billions.

Then there were David and Christopher and April and I. We wore running shoes and torn T-shirts and bits and pieces of clothing from the real world and Everworld. We carried sword and spear and a tiny knife made in a joint venture by the Swiss and a race of aliens from another universe.

In our heads we carried all the assumptions of our own time and place. We believed that planets went around suns, and that deep within our bodies an invisible war raged between germs and viruses and all our physical defenses, that light had a speed and that nothing could exceed it, that energy was mass times the velocity of light squared.

And then there was Senna. She was already a gateway, in a sense. She had both worlds within her. She could explain DNA. She could quote the preamble of the Constitution. She had at least some notion of the Reformation, the Renaissance, the Enlightenment, the Industrial Revolution, the Information Age.

But Senna could also move the course of a river and kill her enemies. And she could feel the presence of a magic tree whose magic roots connected two twinned, crudely opposite worlds within a universe that was not her own.

Stop hating her, Jalil. Stop fearing her. If you want to understand Everworld, understand her. If you hope to hack into the software of this universe, she's your modem.

But how could I not fear her? She had a power I didn't understand. Magic. What was magic? An illusion, a trick, David Copperfield sawing a model in half.

She had moved a river. Without a dam or a shovel she had moved a river. How? How?

Don't fight it, Jalil, I told myself. *Accept it. It's real in this place. It's as real here as all the rules you know from the real world. Don't fight it — learn it, understand it, control it.*

And then take it away from her.

I quickened my pace and slowly drew closer to Senna. Impossible to forget the irritating image of her just coming up out of the river.

It was part of her danger. One of her weapons. She had bewitched David and only released him under threat from Athena. But was I any stronger? Was I immune? Whatever else, I had to avoid letting her make contact with me. Her power was greater when there was direct contact.

Close. Not too close. She saw me. A slight smile, a smirk.

"Hello, Jalil."

"Senna."

"You've come to work on me, have you?"

Already she had me at a disadvantage. Denial would make it worse. "Yes."

"You have questions."

"Yes."

"But you're going to keep your distance."

"Seems like a good idea," I said.

She smiled again. She shivered, shuddered, just a slight thing, but all at once she was naked. Naked and glowing, lit from within, hair a halo of pure gold, eyes no longer gray but vivid blue.

My heart stopped. My pulse seemed to freeze, wait, then hammer back to life. I gasped, amazed. Every cell in my body was electric, sizzling, synapses snapping. I was hungry, a starving man, and all I wanted, needed, all I could even see was this creature, this perfect beauty, every part of me alive and wanting, needing, craving this . . .

It stopped. Cold water in my face. A light switch turned off.

Senna was clothed. Normal. Normal but with a feral, angry mouth and triumphant eyes. "I don't need touch anymore," she said.

Then her eyelids fluttered. For just a moment her eyes lost their alertness, became flat and empty and vague. She drew a deep breath, tried to keep me from noticing it. She recomposed her face.

My body was my own again. I felt lifeless, drained. I felt like a person half dead, shuffling, aimless. But I had kept my eyes on her, watched her, and I knew what she didn't want me to know: The magic tired her. Moving the river had made her fall unconscious. This small illusion that had left indelible marks on my mind had cost her less, but had cost her just the same.

"You've become stronger," I said.

"People grow and change, Jalil." She said it facetiously. Then I guess she decided to change approaches. She switched to a more serious tone. "It's like any other ability, any other talent. If you use it you get better. You get experience. You learn how to feel, how to . . . to position your mind."

"That was impressive with the river."

"Yes, it was, wasn't it? I wasn't sure I could do it."

"You saved our lives."

"I saved my life," she said. "And this mission of ours."

I let that go. I wasn't going to force my gratitude on her. I was distracted by a memory. Recent. Moments old. I felt my body respond and fought it down. Had she hit me again? Or was it just memory?

"Aren't you a little worried about seeing your mother again? It's been a long time, right? Or have you ever even really known her?"

She flushed and clenched her jaw and I thought, *Ah, a little sensitivity there?*

"She's a powerful person, my mother. I look forward to seeing her. Assuming we ever get out of Eshu's fun house and back to the normal Everworld. You and my fool of a half sister have really screwed things up nicely."

I laughed. "We're here because of you, Senna. I could be home minding my own business, leading my own life. You want me to bust out crying because I've made your life uncomfortable?"

"If I wanted you to cry, Jalil, you would. My power is growing. This is my place. This is my time," she said, happy, nodding in satisfaction at the world around her.

"You have a lot of enemies, Senna. And no friends."

I'd meant it to be mean. I guess it was. I think

it hit home, a little at least, because the nice Senna, the civil Senna stepped out of the way then and revealed the cruel young woman beneath the illusion.

"You think you can beat me, Jalil, that's what makes you entertaining," she hissed. "You really think that you can take me apart, take all of this apart, and whip out your calculator and your screwdriver and your tech manual, and control it and me. You sneer at me because you think I lust for power; what do you lust for, Jalil? You want to take this entire universe and make it yours, squeeze it into that little box you have for a brain."

She jerked her chin toward David. "He just wants to be brave, poor, simple thing that he is. Not so much to ask, to be my hero, Athena's hero, your hero. But you, Jalil, you want a power not even Zeus or Odin or Amon-Ra can claim. No wonder you don't believe in God or gods: Thou shalt have no other gods before Jalil."

Yes, I had gotten to her. And she had turned the knife back against me. I quickened my pace and moved away from her, disgusted by her and myself. It was all getting too personal. I shouldn't let that happen. I shouldn't despise Senna. I shouldn't see Eshu as some personal attack. Shouldn't, but did.

We had entered a country of deep-cut rifts, like someone had passed through long, long ago pulling a huge plow and left behind widely spaced furrows. We sidestepped many of the cuts but it was impossible to avoid them all. Which meant climbing, sliding, slipping down into the steep, narrow valley and climbing tediously back up the far side, all the while convinced we were climbing down.

It was hot, miserable work. And the sun was dropping, a blazing red-black eye that grew larger as it neared its illusory intersection with the horizon.

The descents into the valleys were doubly troubling. First because we had no idea what creatures might be lurking there. Second and more unsettling was the distorted sense that we were actually climbing upward into valleys so that I kept trying to use climbing muscles when what I needed were the muscles that slowed descent.

I fell often. So did everyone. The Vikings had our same problem, though they had begun to adapt, having been here longer.

David reached the lip of our current valley, nodded toward the horizon ahead, and said, "That's got to be it."

I struggled up beside him, wiped sweat from

my eyes, and blinked toward the sun. We would not have seen it except that the sun had backlit it to perfection.

Impossible to tell how large it was. But there was nothing on the horizon to remotely touch it. The tree stood alone, surrounded by waving grass turned dark purple by rushing night.

"That is the tree," Senna pronounced. "But it's still a long way off."

"If we get a good moon, we could march through the night," David said, half hopeful-determined and half doleful-weary. No one, not even Thorolf and his men, wanted to keep moving.

We settled down in a waterless place and prepared our thirsty little camp. This time there were more men to gather sharp sticks, but no wood to be found. The valleys were behind us. Nothing could be seen between us and the tree but open space and a stunted, weird threesome of miniaturized giraffes drifting through our field of vision. I almost laughed: short giraffes, that was about the level of the mentality. Senna admired these unseen, unnamed high gods for their simplicity and authenticity. Me, I thought they were just stupid.

David and the Asian Viking took the first watch. Everyone had a weapon and everyone slept with that weapon in hand and boots on. All but Senna, who had no weapon because she was one.

I didn't expect to sleep. But within ten seconds of lying on the cooling ground I was across, back to a gentler if duller world.

that was far in back and moved on. All left work, My Adidas toe kicked a crack in the sidewalk I didn't see as a close up. But with ten seconds stirring up the cool air around a grade school, making a critical mistake as I...

CHAPTER
XX

The Dave Matthews Band. In my headphones. Portable CD player.

My Adidas toe kicked a crack in the sidewalk and I stumbled, stuck my hands out to grab nothing, and landed sprawled on someone's lawn. I jumped up, tried to look cool, but the grass was wet from recent rain and my knees were soaked.

I fought a nausea that washed over me and turned the world upside down briefly. I ripped off the headphones. The world was right side up. Everything was normal, fine.

I took a deep breath. Not a bad CNN: Breaking News. Not the usual tales of imminent horror. Just vertigo carried over from a mind trying to cope with an upside-down world.

"Okay, Jalil. Throw it off. E-Jalil is not your problem right now."

I was on my way to Miyuki's house. She lived two blocks over from Christopher. And speaking of which, there he was, walking along about half a block away. I had parked a good distance away from Miyuki's house. My car was in a somewhat embarrassing condition, having had the left front headlight smashed so that the metal twisted and aimed the shattered lens off to the side. It was not my fault; some idiot had backed into me in the parking lot at school. But it was just the kind of thing Miyuki's dad might jump on. I wasn't going to give the man any ammunition.

Of course now he could notice that my knees were wet. I'd have to walk around for a while, hope they dried. They'd better dry fast; I had maybe three minutes to spare. I was not going to be late. Lateness would be more evidence in Mr. Kuninori's case against me as a lazy, unserious American who wanted to corrupt his daughter with hip-hop, Internet sex, and Saturdays off.

Mr. K. had become my own personal foe. I hadn't met the man, but already he was occupying a large part of my attention.

I'd said I would arrive at six-thirty and I was definitely going to arrive at six-thirty. Not six-thirty-one.

I started to call out to Christopher, a sense of

polite obligation maybe, but I decided against it. We saw enough and more than enough of each other.

Then I noticed something right out of a bad movie: Two guys climbed out of a parked van just as Christopher passed by them. Christopher didn't notice.

Two guys, one of them looked familiar. Like I'd seen him but couldn't remember where. That one was small but walked with a cocky swagger. The second was bigger. Quite a bit bigger. My height but built for football.

Christopher cut down an alleyway. The alleys run parallel to the avenues. That's where people put their garbage cans for pickup, and where most of the garages open up. Christopher was probably looking to reach his car without going through his house.

I lost sight of Christopher. The two guys went right after him and I broke into a run. I don't believe in psychic nonsense or whatever, but I believe in intuition, which is nothing but the rapid analysis of subtle data. My intuition told me this was trouble.

I ran, reached the alleyway, rounded the corner, saw nothing. No one in sight, not Christopher, not the guys. The guy! The guy from the

Taco Bell, what was his name, Kenneth or Kevin or something. Keith, that was it.

I slowed to a more cautious pace. Glanced at my watch. Oh, man. Glanced down at my knees. This really should have been simple. A study date, you show up on time with your books and clean clothes. How hard is that?

A shout. An obscene word. A threat. Then the sickening crunch of something hard on soft flesh.

I jerked forward. There, right in the garage, with its door wide open, there in the shadows, Christopher backed against his dad's car. Keith had a club of some kind, no more than eighteen inches long. Hadn't seen that earlier.

"Hey!" I said sharply.

Keith snapped his eyes toward me. Rage blazed. I saw relief and humiliation on Christopher's face. Keith's backup, the big lummox, just looked confused, a robot without instructions.

Keith said two words, the second of which was "off."

"I don't think so," I said.

In one swift motion, Keith had a gun in his hand, pointed at me. The hole in the end of the barrel looked huge. It filled my entire field of vision, like all the world was collapsed into that round black hole.

"I'd just as soon shoot you as not," Keith said, adding a word I have heard before.

The big ox giggled, a high-pitched sound, like a naughty boy caught filching cookies.

Keith said, "Now, I don't intend to kill my white brother here. I'm just administering a little friendly warning, since I happened to see him talking to a certain detective the other day. But I'll sure kill you."

"That wasn't a cop, you paranoid idiot," Christopher rasped. "I mean, yeah, he's a cop, but he's a friend of my dad's and he was just saying hi."

Keith didn't blink but kept his eyes on me, waiting, looking for an excuse to pull the trigger.

To my surprise I found my voice. It sounded high-strung to me, but I guess it probably sounded controlled enough to Keith. "You're in an alleyway in a nice neighborhood. People saw you come in here. I called my answering machine at home. Used my cell phone." I pointed slowly down at the bulge on my hip. "I called in the license plate of your van. So anything happens to me, it won't take the cops an hour to find you."

It was a bluff, of course. I had a cell phone, that much was true. It could have been true.

The punk's mean eyes narrowed. "What's the license plate number? If you called it in, you must still remember it."

I rattled off the number. He blinked.

"You're one of the smart ones, huh?" he sneered.

"That's right. I'm one of the smart ones."

He bit his lip, lowered the gun, slid it under his jacket, very hard-ass gangster. He'd learned his moves from TV.

"Any word of this to the cops and it won't matter if I get busted. I'll pop a cap on you." He nodded, grinned savagely at Christopher. "You, too."

They walked away. The big one was careful to slam me with a shoulder as he passed.

I stepped inside the garage, and Christopher hit the button to lower the door.

"So. I guess you're wondering what that's about, huh?"

I didn't say anything. I just enjoyed the fact that I was still breathing. Although now I was getting mad. Anger was growing geometrically, doubling in size every few seconds.

"Look," Christopher said, "it's this stupid job I had, the one at the copy shop? The one I got fired from? Those guys are from there. They're like some Aryan Nazi whatevers. Nuts."

"Why are they after you? What did you do?"

He shrugged. "I didn't want to join up. They took it personally."

I nodded tightly. "But they thought you might want to join?"

"Hey, don't start that crap, all right, Jalil? I'm having a bad day here." He rubbed his bruised ribs.

"Yeah, and now your bad day is my bad day, so don't try and blow me off. That little psycho had a gun on me, so don't tell me you don't want to talk about it or whatever and feed me some half-assed story."

He bit his lip, looked down at the floor of the garage. "Look, I'm not one of those guys, okay? Maybe I'm politically incorrect. Maybe I make jokes I shouldn't make. That doesn't make me one of those guys."

"Uh-huh. And yet, they thought you might be."

He looked pissed. He was about to fire off a smart comeback. His mouth opened, then closed. He sighed and shook his head. "Yeah. They figured maybe I was like them. They figured maybe I was ready to sign up for white power and all that crap."

"Okay."

"I was never like that, Jalil. I never hated people. I wasn't like that." He was trying to reassure himself as much as me. "I was always just talk. And I'm not like that anymore. Mostly," he added ruefully.

I believed him. I was busting him, but basically I believed him.

"I have a question for you," I said, calmer now the adrenaline was settling down in my blood. "What do we do about this? About these guys?"

"We can't kick their butts. I mean, we can, but Keith is a hopelessly messed up little Kip Kinkle–Dylan Klebold wanna-be. He's nuts and he won't scare because he's just too crazy to care."

"He's not the brains, right? I mean, I assume there's someone over him."

"Yeah. Mr. Trent."

"Well, my guess is that Keith is not afraid to do time. I'm sure he'd see it as being a martyr for the cause. But by the same token I'd guess your friend Mr. Trent is a little more cautious. As a rule the soldiers do the dying while the officers sit back and give out the orders."

Christopher agreed cautiously.

"So we go to the cops, file a charge for what just happened here. They arrest Keith. Mr. Trent will tell Keith to back off because if Keith tries anything the heat will increase and Mr. Trent will get burned. If we say nothing we're just Keith's fools. He can jack us up any time he feels like it."

Christopher winced. Unsure, but too humbled to resist much. "Yeah. Yeah, that's probably right. Trent thinks he's Adolf himself. He's not going down for Keith. But Keith will take a bullet for Trent."

I said, "Yeah, that's the math, the way I see it."

He sucked in a deep breath. "Call the cops, huh?"

"Call that detective you said was a friend of your dad. That way we get a fair hearing before they decide they better handcuff me just on general principles."

Christopher looked a bit brighter at that prospect. "Yeah, yeah. I'll call him. He's cool. Yeah, that's it, Jalil, that's what we do. You're right." He grinned his old taunting grin. "But then, you're one of the smart ones."

"Yeah, I'm smart. I've just blown my date with Miyuki, probably permanently. I lose the possible love of my life to save your sorry ass. I'm a genius, that's what I am. Let's make the call before Keith realizes I was bluffing about the license plate."

CHAPTER
XXI

I woke to see David's face in mine.

"What?" I asked, bleary.

"You're on, man. Nothing happening, but it's your watch."

"Oh. Yeah." I rubbed my eyes with the heels of my hands.

"Maybe Christopher would switch if you're not up for it," David suggested, nodding toward Christopher asleep by the fire and nearly spooning with one of the Chinese Viking.

"No. I'll do it. I'm up. Christopher's having a bad day over there."

"In the real world?"

I stood up, stretched, yawned, resisted the desire to cringe and grab handfuls of grass lest I fall into the starry sky. "Yeah. We're now screwed in two universes. Christopher's been making some bad friends."

I gave David the short version of the story. If anything unfortunate happened to me in the real world, the more people who knew the facts, the better.

David looked pissed off more than worried. He called Christopher a name. Not the worst name, but not a term of endearment, either.

"He's coming around," I said in Christopher's defense. "He's joining the human race. Little by little."

David nodded, still pissed. It was one more factor for the general to consider. One more uncontrollable variable. I told him he could take off, grab some Z's. But he didn't leave.

"Jalil, man, you ever think maybe there's some . . . I don't know the word, some, like, osmosis or whatever? I mean between the two universes. Like maybe some of this world bleeds through to there?"

I looked hard at him. "You have something to tell me?"

He seemed annoyed that I was pushing him. But then he made a wry smile. "Remind me not to try and BS you. Yeah, something. This woman. I met her by accident when I pulled off the road coming down Sheridan. One of those mansions. She said something about 'closing the gateway.' "

"Not the computer."

He shook his head. "No. I figured she was a maid. That's how she looked." I shrugged. "Tried to believe she was just talking about the gate, you know? Close the gate to the driveway, but that didn't make any sense."

I felt a chill. The night was far colder than it should have been, given the heat of the day. "You think what, exactly? You think that woman is connected to this? What else? Wait a minute, you think this Keith creep is connected to this."

He made a deprecating face. "What do I know, Jalil? I'm not the guy to figure this out. Maybe I'm just putting two and two together and coming up with five. I'm just saying this Keith guy seems to have too big a hard-on for Christopher, given what happened. Why is he threatening Christopher? I mean, if he wanted to keep Christopher quiet, he's going at it the wrong way. You guys are over there right now giving him up."

"And the woman with the gateway?"

"I don't know. I'm paranoid, that's all. Tired, too. I'm going to cross over."

"Yeah. Hey, am I supposed to wake one of the Vikings?"

"Nah. They don't seem to be too determined on staying awake. Of course, they're trying to die." He walked off, turned, and added, "Hey, by the way, that snuffling sound you'll hear is just hyenas out in the dark. I think."

I chafed my hands together, trying to warm them. I couldn't see the big tree. I couldn't see anything. The fire burned low, and in any case its light didn't penetrate three feet beyond the outer ring of sleeping men.

I heard animal sounds. Low growls. Scuffling. Movement. I couldn't see but had an impression of creatures in the dark, moving in a restless circle around us. Attracted but afraid.

I should be thinking about tomorrow. I should be working on a plan. But how could I? I didn't know how to get out of this upside-down place. At one level it was just one damned thing too many. Not enough to be trapped in an alternate universe? We had to be trapped in a mirror-image of an alternate universe?

How to bust out? How to escape? Eshu was the key. How could I beat Eshu without giving him what he demanded?

Should be easy. What was he, after all? Some low-rent semigod who was fixated on sacrifices.

All at once, without fanfare or announcement, there he was. He was standing by the fire, back to the flames, warming his butt, hands clasped behind him. Don King on Weight Watchers.

I looked around. Everyone was asleep. Snores, some soft, some like saws working on knotty wood. I wished April were awake.

"What do you want?" I asked Eshu.

"You are very stubborn," he said.

"Maybe so."

"Why not just make the sacrifice? I can arrange for a sheep to appear. It is a simple thing. The Orisha and the great high gods are angry with you, but they can be appeased."

He seemed like the soul of reason. A wise old man talking to a hotheaded young fool.

"Listen, old man, or old god, or whatever you are, it's not just a sheep. You want me to bend my knee to you and your so-called high gods. I don't do that. Not as long as I can still think."

He looked curiously at me. "Why do you deny the gods their due? This is their land. My land. If you come into my land is your life not mine to dispose of as I please?"

"No. It's not."

"But you are mortal. Mortals live or die at the pleasure of the gods. As a slave is to his owner, thus is a mortal to his gods."

"You said it."

Eshu looked honestly perplexed. I didn't sense that he was taking pleasure in threatening us. In bringing on hideous nightmares. In launching attacks of demons. I didn't see a sadist there. Just a god operating according to rules he thought were perfectly obvious.

"You will leave the Orisha with no choice but to kill you. My brothers and sisters will have your obedience or your life."

"Yeah? You and your team haven't managed to kill all these Vikings yet, and they're looking to die."

Now that was stupid. I was daring him to kill us.

Eshu shook his head slowly, regretfully. And then he was gone and I was left blinking at the night and wondering whether it had been a dream or real or whether, in this nuthouse, there was any difference.

After a while I roused Christopher, who grumbled that we had spent three hours giving statements to the cops and that an FBI guy had driven up from Chicago and made us do it all over again.

I wondered if I was right about going to the cops. If David's suspicion was correct, maybe Keith was operating on a whole different plane.

"I've seen enough cops to hold me for a while," Christopher said through his yawns.

"Yeah," I agreed. But then a thought occurred

to me. "You know, though, we could use a few in this universe."

Christopher barked out a laugh that caused Senna to stir. "Cops would be a start. Marines would be even better. And if that doesn't clean this place up, bring on the assistant principals."

In the morning a pure white lamb stood calmly unafraid, just outside the circle of our camp.

I thought maybe David or Senna or certainly Christopher would go for it. But no one broke ranks. I guess the message was a bit too pointed. People's backs were up now. Even Christopher was in a "screw you, Eshu" frame of mind.

I knew it was a mistake, that was the hell of it. I knew I'd let it all get personal, that I was making decisions that were more emotional than rational. And — with some help from April — I'd managed to get us all into a confrontation we were unlikely to win.

Too late. What could I do, announce that I was switching sides? I would lose all my credibility.

Besides, truth was, I couldn't do that. I couldn't let Eshu beat me.

We marched toward the tree. North-shore teenagers looking for a permanent way home and Vikings looking for a belated ticket to Valhalla.

And of course, our witch.

I intended to use her. I wasn't sure if she'd let me, wasn't sure if I could force her. And I wasn't sure if Eshu could stop me.

I didn't like what I was thinking. I didn't like having to wonder whether I should tell Senna, or find some way to force her against her will.

Well, Jalil, I told myself, *you fight with the weapons you have.* If you had a chainsaw or a bulldozer or a flamethrower you'd use them. Instead, you have a witch. So use the witch. Win the battle. Then worry about the right and the wrong. Not like she didn't deserve it. Not like she hadn't used us.

Maybe that was a bonus. A part of me was grinning a nasty grin, teeth bared, greedy for Senna's humiliation. A part of me was laughing at her, taunting her, thinking that I would do to her what she had done to me.

Too much emotion in all this, another part of me warned. You're settling scores, Jalil; that's never a good idea.

The tree was big, beyond any normal tree. Like three or four redwoods, although not so much tall as wide and full. But it wasn't big on the scale of some things in Everworld. This tree wasn't big the way the Midgard Serpent was a big snake, or the way Nidhoggr was big. It was huge, but huge in a sort of modest way.

It did stand out, all alone in a sea of blue and orange grass. Nothing but grass approached it. A herd of elephants seemed to go out of its way to avoid the tree's shade.

There wasn't so much a sense of threat from the tree. More like an air of importance. The elephants didn't turn their backs to the tree, or run from it. They just wandered wide of it. An elephant's version of respect, maybe.

But we were going right for the tree. It grew larger and larger. Closer. And the feeling of it grew in me. The feeling that I was seeing something old and vital and magnificent. A work of ancient art. A Colosseum or a Parthenon or a Notre Dame de Paris.

The tree united the two halves of this African world. The familiar world and the simplistically backward underworld. Senna had felt the roots beneath her some miles away from the tree itself. They formed the arteries and veins of this twinned world.

David fell back to match step with me. "Okay, you have some kind of plan?"

I nodded. Glanced meaningfully at Senna and together David and I wandered away from her. Thorolf saw and joined in.

"Yonder is the great tree," Thorolf said. "It weighs down my heart."

David said, "Well, that's supposed to be what connects this upside-down world with the regular world."

Thorolf nodded. "Just as Yggdrasil carries the weight of all the worlds on its roots and branches."

"Uh-huh. That's just what I was thinking," David said dryly. "So what's the big plan?"

Thorolf looked at me, surprised at the notion that I would be formulating a plan.

Me, I was just surprised at the nature of the plan. I said, "Senna. When she got cut back there, her blood ran down all over her foot. Wherever she stepped, wherever she bled, the grass died."

David jerked his head back, like I'd said something offensive. "What are you talking about?"

"Her blood. It's toxic."

"Witch's blood is deadly poison," Thorolf agreed, stating a commonplace, like he was confirming that too much sugar would rot your teeth. "A witch must be strangled or burned or drowned. You never cut the head from a witch or her blood will render all the land sterile. Just try growing a fine crop of rye or wheat in soil where a witch's blood has been shed."

He got a faraway look. "I wonder how the crop was this year. My good woman will do her best; she's a hard worker. But I should have liked to look out over my fields one last time."

"I liked your farm," I said.

He nodded gratefully. "It is a fine farm. Although I wish I could have bred the bull and . . ." He sighed, shook his head ruefully. "Well, I was lucky enough to die a warrior's death in battle. Thank the gods I did not die tending my fields, an old used-up man. That would have meant an afterlife in Hel. The sagas paint a grim picture of Hel."

"The sagas don't know the half of it," David said grimly. He patted the Viking on the shoulder. "We'll get you back to the real world. I don't guess you'll see your fields again, but you'll see Valhalla."

Thorolf brightened up, grinned, laughed, his eyes twinkling. "The finest ale ever brewed, and your cup never runs dry. Of course, you could drink the water! Ah-ha-ha-ha!"

It was impossible not to smile when Thorolf laughed. He was one of those guys. I felt a pang and knew that I would miss him when he was truly dead. Those hectic, scary days with the Vikings already seemed like the "good old days."

The Viking spotted one of his men leering a little too blatantly at April and moved off to deliver a friendly Viking warning in the form of a backhand slap that would have knocked my head clear off my neck.

The nostalgia went with him. David was glaring at me, eyes murderous. "Have you talked to Senna about this?" he demanded.

I shook my head. "No. She may not go along."

"Jesus, Jalil. You know what you're talking about?"

"I'm talking about killing that big tree there," I said. "Maybe killing the flip side of it, too, maybe destroying the cohesion of this messed-up little world here. Maybe killing a bunch of people, animals, a whole way of life."

David was taken aback. He'd been thinking only about Senna. "Kind of a high price to pay, isn't it? All that so you don't have to bow down? You bowed to Loki. You bowed to Hel. Suddenly you're Mr. Integrity?"

"Those were different. I was giving way to superior force. I had no choice. This is different. Eshu wants me to bend. He wants me to give up what I believe. He wants me to submit on my own." I wasn't even convincing myself. I felt I had to add something, so lamely I said, "Besides, April won't do it."

"Uh-huh. So it's a personal thing, you and Eshu. He messed with you and now you're determined to show him who's boss. You and April both, for that matter."

"I can beat him," I snapped.

David didn't answer.

"We'll bluff him. He'll fold," I said.

"And if he doesn't? Or if she stops you?"

"You going to back me or not?" I demanded. "I've backed you plenty, David. I backed you when you were Senna's bitch, David."

He didn't flare up like I expected. He fidgeted with the hilt of his sword. He was in a box. He had no plan of his own. And it was true that I had backed him up many times. And he couldn't look, even now, like he was Senna's puppet. That last thing was what I counted on: This was David's chance to make it clear once and for all that he was no longer Senna's tool.

"Damn you, Jalil," he said. "I'll back you up."

That should have been a relief. But it meant the sick plan I had hatched in my head was about to become real. And how would my friends here look at me afterward?

I stared straight ahead, right at the tree. I had boasted that I would figure out the software. I had said I'd hack into Everworld and work the rules to my own ends. Well, here was the chance. Real-world reason meets Everworld magic.

Yeah, Jalil, tell yourself that's all there is to it. Tell yourself it's not personal. It's not ego. Real-world reason meets magic? No, real-world, nuclear-age ruthlessness meets Everworld naïveté.

Come on, Eshu. You think this is your land? You want to see me bend my knee? Come on, old man, I'm taking you to school.

CHAPTER
XXIII

The tree's trunk was a skyscraper. Not the Sears Tower, maybe, but one of those lesser towers. Big enough to house a few dozen law firms, accountants, an insurance company, and room for a Starbucks and Subway on the ground floor.

It was possible to imagine a bigger tree, but that didn't change the fact that this was one big tree. All of it was on a larger scale. The lower branches were as thick as big sewer pipes. The bark itself was like the armor plates of dinosaurs, a rough brickwork.

Any strong person would be able to climb it. Footholds, handholds, awkward and dangerous, but doable.

We stood there, our ragged troop, all gazing up at branches that could have hosted squirrels the size of rhinoceroses. I half expected to find ants as big as cats crawling in single file up the trunk.

I glanced at David. He looked grim, gray. But he gave a curt nod. My heart skipped several beats.

So this was what it was like to be in charge. To make the decisions David usually made. A weird mix of excitement and power rush and fear and vulnerability. I felt sick.

I took out Excalibur, my Coo-Hatch knife. I opened the blade. I walked up the gradual slope of an exposed root, balanced my way along, fighting the vertigo, closing my eyes from time to time just to clear away the illusion that I was an ant crawling suspended beneath a massive root that formed a ceiling.

I advanced till I was ten feet up in the air, up where the root joined the trunk. Then I began cutting. I made a long vertical slice, from as high as I could reach, all the way down between my feet. I stretched back up and made a parallel slice.

"Jalil, man, what are you doing, carving, 'Jalil loves Miyuki'?" Christopher asked.

"No. I'm going to kill this tree."

"Kill the tree?" Christopher laughed. "When? Sometime around the turn of the next century? It's a two-inch blade and a tree the size of —"

David struck. His sword came up and out of its sheath. He swung the pommel hard. The gold and steel made a sickening crunch as it hit the back of Senna's head.

Senna's face registered shock, then her eyes rolled up. She collapsed.

"What the hell?" Christopher yelled.

"David, what are you doing?" April cried.

Even the Vikings were stunned.

David knelt to check the already-swelling knot on Senna's head. His hands came away smeared with blood. He wiped it off with a handful of grass. Then he showed the grass to April and Christopher. The stems were withering, twisting.

David threw the grass away. He looked heartsick. I guess I did, too.

I turned back to my work. I began making a series of shorter horizontal slashes in the root and lower trunk. As I cut I explained, falsely calm, pedantic. "These cuts will let the poison through the bark, into the veins of the tree. The poison will spread throughout the whole tree."

"No. This is wrong, Jalil." April. My ally.

I stopped what I was doing, turned carefully, not wanting to fall. April was white-faced, shocked, scared.

I said, "It's not going to hurt Senna."

"You're going to kill this tree?" April demanded.

"Are you crazy? You know this tree is supposedly holding all this together — what about all the people who live here? You don't know how much damage you may do."

"Come on, David," I said coldly, ignoring April, ignoring the part of me that agreed with her.

David put his arms around Senna, hauled her up off the ground, lifted her up like a groom carrying his bride across the threshold.

Thorolf stepped up and took part of the weight. He took her legs and David her arms. Senna hung like a killed deer being carried off by hunters.

Christopher looked uncertain. His eyes darted from April to me. Pleading, wanting someone to tell him what to do. Then, with a helpless look for April, he came to help balance David and Thorolf as they climbed the root.

Eshu appeared. I was expecting him. But he looked different. Younger. Stronger. No longer playing the simple old man. He was revealed now as a powerfully built warrior, perhaps twenty-five. The hair was the same, but now he radiated vital energy.

And then, around the tree below us, other figures materialized. Terrible creatures, male and female.

A massive, powerful man with fire in his nostrils, whose every breath made thunder rumble . . . a young-looking man, not much older than me, but with a body divided in half, vertically, white on one side, black on the other . . . a woman who seemed to be made of water, suspended, muddy liquid. Her ears, neck, lips, arms were all adorned with fantastic copper bracelets and baubles . . . a nightmarish figure covered with open, running sores, bleeding pockmarks . . . a figure with the head of a lion . . . a figure with the head of a demon . . .

"The Orisha," I said.

"Those who you have insulted," Eshu snapped.

"Keep moving," I grated to David.

Senna's inert body was closer to the sliced bark.

"Get down from the tree," Eshu warned.

David manhandled Senna up, grabbed her by her dress, and pushed her against the tree trunk. He held her there and I grabbed her right leg with one hand and held the knife against her flesh.

The blade that would cut anything was an inch from a vein in Senna's ankle.

"Let us go, Eshu," I said with cold triumph. "Let us go, or I'll spill this witch's blood into the tree."

Eshu hesitated. I thought, *I have him. I have the bastard.*

Then I saw a look in the god's eyes that I recognized: defiance. He wasn't going to be beaten. Not by me. Whatever the risk.

All at once the sensation that had dogged us all, the feeling that we were upside down and the world was upside down, that the sky was below us and the ground above, all of that became real. Gravity reversed.

I fell toward the sky. Senna, David, we all fell upward/downward, fell up/down into the tree branches that were above us.

I fell toward the white sky and blue clouds.

I hit a branch. Hit it with my lower back, kidneys and muscles slammed, pain like a cattle prod. I swarmed, tried to grab on, hold, slipped, fell, bellowed in terror and rage, fell, slammed again, this time twisted, grabbed, fingers scrabbling, feet kicking.

I was on a branch, holding on with one arm and the weight of my own body bent over the branch, guts heaving. I gasped for air, lungs collapsed, empty, sucked in a breath.

I looked up toward the ground above. The Orisha stood there, implacable, upside down, standing as though nothing had happened. Standing upside down, glued to the dirt and grass sky, gazing up at me, Eshu with cold triumph.

I glanced down toward the sky, toward the higher branches of the tree. Far, far off, far below I saw three figures twisting, turning, silent-screaming as they fell forever and ever. One of them —

the Asian Viking, I thought — hit a cloud, puffed baby blue, and disappeared from sight.

In the branches, here and there, the others. Vikings. Thorolf. And, I hoped, my friends. I couldn't see Christopher but I could hear him cursing violently. I neither saw nor heard April.

David was just below me. He had one arm wrapped around a branch. His body hung in air, and with his other hand he held a still unconscious Senna, a limp rag doll with hair that moved fitfully in the breeze.

David was losing his grip on the branch. I knew he'd fall before he'd let go of Senna. I had to reach him. But the vertigo, the confusion, the mind warp was twisting my perceptions. I literally could not figure out how to move, which way. I forced concentration, ignored the pain in my pummeled body.

Toward the sky. Up. Down. No, forget those words, they mean nothing. I looked away from the tree. A herd of gazelles alternately leaped and moped along, a quarter mile away, upside down, indifferent to the fact that for us gravity had been reversed on orders from a skinny minor god.

I inched along the branch toward the trunk. Grab the rough bark, Jalil, use it, just like climbing one of those mountain-climbing walls. Except for there being no safety line. Except for the fact that if I slipped I wouldn't fall twenty feet to a padded floor, I'd fall forever and ever into an empty sky.

I closed my eyes, yelled, "David, hang on, I'm coming."

I reached his branch, slid out onto it.

"Hurry," he gritted.

No time for caution. No time to crawl. I sucked in a deep breath, winced at the pain in my ribs, and stepped forward onto the branch, tightrope walking. It was the balance beam event at the Olympics. Five steps at a near run, then I dropped down, hugged the branch for a second, reached, and grabbed David around the armpit.

I had him but I had nowhere near the strength to pull him up. All I could do was keep him from slipping any farther.

"Let her go," I said.

"No."

"I can't pull you both up, David."

"Not letting her go," he said in a near-sob.

"Christopher!" I yelled. "Get here. We need help!"

"Where are you?"

"Senna! Wake up!" David cried.

I yelled, "Below . . . I mean, we're, I think we're toward the sky. I can't see you. Can you reach the trunk? Maybe you can see us from there. Hurry."

Eshu appeared. He squatted comfortably on the branch just beyond David.

"Mortals must learn to respect the gods," he said smugly. "You must make a sacrifice; you must show respect."

"All right," David snapped. "Damn it, Jalil, give it up. It's over."

Eshu gloated, grinned at me, deliberately provocative.

"David's our leader," I said tightly. "If he orders me to do it, I'll do it." It was a cowardly way out. I was giving in; I was submitting and trying to blame it on David. I had never considered anything David said to be an order. It was a pathetic, self-justifying lie. It was all I had.

"Do it!" David said.

"Bring on your sheep," I said to Eshu.

He grinned, nasty, hard, coldly angry. "Sheep? No. The time has passed for offering sheep."

"Then what the hell do you want?" I raged. "You win, all right? What do you want?"

"The witch," he hissed. "Kill the witch. Strangle the life from her and offer her life to the gods."

CHAPTER XXIV

My insides turned to ice.

"What?"

A blur of movement, a flying creature the size of a lion, but with the unmistakable roar of a Viking berserker. Thorolf dropped, hit Eshu, wrapped his beefy arms around him and knocked the messenger of the gods into the sky.

They fell, twirling toward the clouds.

"Ha-ha-ha, by Mighty Thor's hammer, I have you!" Thorolf exulted, voice fading away as he fell/rose.

Eshu pushed, writhed, punched, but Thorolf held him close, wrapped him up in his python arms.

I yelled, "Get ready, he'll reverse gravity to save himself!"

It was instantaneous. Up became down. I'd

just had time to scuttle around the branch, beneath it, and now I was above it again, and the ground was down while seeming up, and the sky was up while seeming to be down. Eshu and Thorolf were a cannonball reaching the top of its arc. They slowed, stopped, began to fall back down toward the tree.

I heard Christopher yell. I heard April scream.

I grabbed at David, we scrambled madly, heaved at anything we could grab, and then, a gasping rest as the two of us and Senna were finally safely draped across a branch with gravity pulling us down.

Eshu and Thorolf blew past, slowed, and landed with minimal impact on the grass below us.

Thorolf still held the god. He looked like some WWF freak who had grabbed a skinny guy up out of the audience and was intent on squeezing him till his eyes popped.

The other Orisha looked nonplussed. But now Eshu was shape-shifting, becoming a lion. Not even Thorolf could hold a lion.

"We're above the slash marks," I said to David.

"Tell them," he snapped.

"Eshu! Eshu!" I cried. I grabbed Senna's ankle and pressed my knife against it again. "I'll cut. She'll bleed. And your tree will wither and die.

Along with you and the rest of your little freak show."

He stopped changing. He was a thin old man again. A man in a loincloth with Don King's hair. He glared up at me, seething with dangerous rage. I swear he would never have given way. I swear I saw intransigence, suicidal stubbornness in his eyes.

But then his expression softened, his gaze became vague. He seemed to be listening. He nodded slowly and bowed his head.

For a while he said nothing. He was swallowing his personal rage. Swallowing his own will. Just what he had made me do.

At last he met my gaze again, and now he was perfectly composed, calm, accepting. "The great high gods have spoken," he said. "You may leave this world."

It was sudden and complete. The sky was no longer white but blue. The clouds were puffy cotton. The grass was green and yellow and definitely below us.

Also below us, Eshu. All the other Orisha had gone. Evaporated. Had they ever even been there?

Senna was stirring, waking up, moaning. David and I handed her down as gently as we could.

April appeared below us and helped her half sister down to the grass.

Christopher came around the trunk of the tree. The Vikings milled together, looking spooked.

"Are we free to go?" David asked Eshu.

I couldn't gloat. Didn't feel like it anyway. I had been ready to submit. Eshu had lost, and yet he'd beaten me, too. We were two scarred, wounded veterans from different sides of a pointless battle.

"You may go," Eshu said. "The sacrifices have appeased the high gods."

"What sacrifices?" April demanded.

An impact that shook the ground. I jerked my head, saw the Viking bounce. Another impact, another. The three Vikings who had fallen into a white sky fell out of a blue one and slammed the earth. None ever moved.

Eshu grinned. "The great high gods have all wisdom. I am only their humble messenger."

"Screw you, too," I said.

Eshu laughed and turned away. Without looking back he said, "Do not come to this land again."

"Yeah," I agreed.

He was gone. And I was left feeling my ribs to see if any of them were broken.

But my own aches and pains and bruises were nothing now. Because now the Vikings all around us were bleeding, gushing red, guts spilling. One man's head fell cleanly off his neck.

As I stared, horrified, a long, bloody gash opened up in Thorolf's chest.

He gaped down at it, seemed frightened for a moment, then smiled and said, "Ah."

"Is that . . . is that the wound that killed you?" April asked gently.

He nodded. "Yes. And here it is again. Already I feel cold death approaching."

The Vikings were dropping, falling, moaning. Dying around us of their renewed wounds. It was the aftermath of battle, all condensed, all so sudden. Bloody yet nearly silent.

Thorolf staggered, fell to his knees. April went to him, put her hand on his shoulder. He smiled at her, then pushed her away.

"I die a warrior!" he yelled in his usual roar. "Come to me, Valkyries! Come to Thorolf. I claim a warrior's right!"

Then he fell onto his face. David felt the pulse in his neck. He patted the Viking's pot-metal helmet.

"He's dead."

"They're all dead," Senna said.

I was startled to hear her. Did she know what we'd done to her? What I had done to her?

I composed my face and looked at her. Oh, yes.

She knew. She knew, and if she meant to frighten me she did a good job. No rage, no tantrum, just cool, controlled, determined malevolence. She had never been a friend. Now she was an enemy.

"I hope the Valkyries have him," Christopher said. "I hope he made it to Valhalla."

All at once, as if in answer to his sentiment, the entire sky ripped open. Four women astride four massive horses appeared in the sky, galloping on air, blond braids flying, swords slapping against bare, muscular thighs. Their faces were stern, not beautiful so much as flawless. They had crazy-wild blue eyes and bared their teeth like sharks closing in on a surfer. They were armed and armored and helmeted, and any one of them could have put her fist through a brick wall. They made Xena look like a member of the Baby-sitters Club.

Then it was as if the blue sky were theater curtains. The Valkyries grabbed handfuls of blue and rolled it back to reveal an amazing scene. We were standing just outside of an impossibly vast room. The timbers that supported the roof were as big as the tree that still shaded us. There were rows of high, arched windows you could have flown a 747 through, and tables that were thousands of feet long, but narrow enough to reach across.

And everywhere, everywhere, thousands, tens of thousands, maybe more Vikings, all dressed in fabulous furs and glittering golden armor, gnashed their teeth on joints of meat as big as Virginia hams, and raised massive silver cups and swilled rivers of pale yellow ale.

The noise was deafening: shouts, roars, bellows, boasts, good-natured threats, banged cups, food flung and chewed and ripped. It was a wall of noise.

And there, standing nearest to us, was Thorolf. Not far off I spotted Olaf Ironfoot and Sven Swordeater, two of the Vikings we'd seen die while fighting the Aztecs.

Valhalla.

"Okay, that's the frat I'm rushing when I get to college," Christopher said with an amazed laugh.

"Ah! My minstrels!" Thorolf yelled happily. "I've told my brothers of your great song, my minstrel friends. They demand to hear it sung." He swilled a cup and turned to bellow in a voice that should have made my ears bleed, "Listen up, you dogs! Listen to the song of the minstrels!"

"The song?" April echoed. "For all of them?"

But what were we going to do? Say no to a hundred thousand drunken Vikings, all of whom had died in battle? Say no to our friend Thorolf? Say no to the glowering Valkyries?

So we sang the song we had sung for Olaf and Thorolf so long ago.

We were shaky at first, struggling to pick up the tune and get into the same key. Straining at some of the half-remembered lyrics. But we sang it.

"Mine eyes have seen the glory of the mighty Viking lords, they are trampling out the vineyards where the grapes of wrath are stored. They have loosed the fateful lightning of their terrible swift swords. The Vikes are marching on!"

"Glory, glory hallelujah, lordy how we'll stick it to ya. Glory, glory hallelujah, the Vikes are marching on!"

By the second verse we were warmed up and laughing as we sang.

"We jumped aboard our longboats and sailed upon the seas, and we slaughtered all who fought us, and we did just as we pleased, 'cause we're crazy Viking warriors and we never beg for peace, the Vikes are marching on!"

In the history of the world no one ever got the kind of hand we got. The Vikings didn't politely applaud. They erupted into what looked an awful lot like a full-fledged riot. They shook their weapons and howled, and the Valkyries joined in, shrieking horribly and twirling their swords and spears.

And then we sang the song again. And again. And only after the entire drunken crowd was singing along did Thorolf nod to us and say, "Thank you, my minstrel friends."

"Thank you, Thorolf," I whispered.

And Christopher yelled, "Hey, Thorolf. So how is the beer in Valhalla?"

Thorolf threw back his big head and laughed, "Ha-ha-ha!" and drained about a gallon down his throat.

The Valkyries drew the curtains of sky closed, slipped through the seam, and disappeared completely.

For a long time no one said anything.

Then David sighed. "The Coo-Hatch are with us again. Way back there."

"And Egypt is that way," Senna said.

EVER WORLD

#IX

INSIDE THE ILLUSION

"What is this, Planet of the Zombies?" April wondered. "This place gives me the creeps. There's no noise."

"Look, kitties!" Jalil said.

"Kitties?" Christopher repeated. "Did you just say 'kitties'?"

"Cats. I said cats," Jalil amended. "Look, there, by that doorway."

At least a dozen cats lounged comfortably on a slab of sun-warmed stone beside a doorway that could have easily admitted a dinosaur.

"Hey, look, there are more up there." April pointed. "And there. Jeez. A lot of cats."

They were easy to overlook at first in the shadow of skyscraper slabs of stone. But once noticed, they seemed to be everywhere.

"Anyone ever see *The Birds*? All these seagulls

go nuts and start killing people?" Christopher asked nervously. "These kitties look like bad kitties."

April laughed. "There's no such thing as a bad kitty. Didn't the ancient Egyptians treat them like gods? Here, kitty. Here, kitty kitty."

Jalil said, "You know, watch what you say. They may be able to talk."

"W.T.E.," Christopher agreed. "Welcome To Everworld."

April diverted toward a cluster of cats in the shadow of a stone lion. Then she stopped, froze, and let go with a scream that jerked the Amazons around, swords at the ready.

Merope was in full combat mode and David not a split second behind her. Then Merope laughed. "Oh, that." She sheathed her sword and shook her head in amused contempt.

April rejoined us, shaken, white-faced, hands wringing.

"What was it?" David demanded, still not sure he should relax.

"The cats. They were . . . There's a dead person over there. The cats are eating him. . . ."